CAT(
MANCHESTER

by
Bill Rogers

CATON

Caton Books Ltd

April 2014

ISBN 978-1-909856-13-4

Contents

Foreword		6
Introduction		7
Walk 1	Around Deansgate	11
Walk 2	Around the Cathedral Gardens	29
Walk 3	Chinatown and the Gay Village	38
Walk 4	Castlefield Urban Heritage Park.	51
Walk 5	Salford Quays and The Lowry	62
Walk 6	Around the Universities – The Cultural Corridor.	71
Walk 7	Debdale Park and The Monastery and Friary of St Francis, Gorton.	87
Walk 8	West Pennines Country Park - Rivington	98
Acknowledgements		105
Useful Links		106
The Author		107

Foreword

A great deal of care was taken in preparing the walks in this book. This included walking each route, visiting every venue identified, and physically checking access to streets, and buildings. All of the details in this book were accurate, to the best of the publisher's knowledge, as of 14th April 2014. Any subsequent changes of access to roads, streets or buildings, to transport routes or timetables, admission times and prices for museums, galleries, and attractions, are beyond the publisher's control, and no responsibility can be accepted for any consequent inconvenience or injury. The prudent traveller will always check such details in advance of their walk, and will take care when crossing roads and tramways.

Introduction

I had the seed of an idea for this book of walks way back when I began to write The Cleansing, the first of what has become the DCI Tom Caton Murder Mysteries.

Caton, my protagonist, was born in Manchester, grew up there, went to school at Chorlton High School, and Manchester Grammar School where he was a member of the Local History Society, and studied for his degree and postgraduate qualifications at Manchester University. He is passionate about Manchester. Having been orphaned in his teens, it is more than just a city to him. It is his home, and his family. That this should be reflected in the novels was a given. But he was not the only one. I too was born and raised in a city, but not this one.

I confess. I am not a Manc. I was born within the sound of Bow Bells. I am a Londoner. But that means that I too have a passion for cities. I understand something about the pull of the city, the history, and the beating heart. The ways in which a city changes, yet stays the same. That in reality a city is a series of villages, each of whose occupants have a fierce pride in their locality, yet an equal passion for the city as a whole. I understand the way in which allegiance to a city football team - in my case Arsenal, in Caton's case Manchester City, and in my wife's Manchester United - can unite people across those diverse 'villages', and can divide a family.

When I came 'North' in 1966, to marry and settle down, it was inevitable that I should be drawn to the city of Manchester, and to fall in love with it. Specifically, with its history, its culture, its compact, bustling and diverse physical presence, its confident determination, and its people.

During the 18 years when I had the privilege to work for the City Council Education Department, essentially for the children and young people, their parents, carers and teachers, I came to know the city even more intimately. Throughout that time my 'Head Office' was in the city centre in Crown Square, overlooking the Crown Courts. My first task was to enter the police cells there to suspend a teacher who had been accused of dealing drugs from the back of the school minibus during a school camp. But I was also based for significant periods of time in Harper Hey, in Moss Side, and in Royal Oak. My work took me across the city into every school, college and all three Universities. Into nurseries and playgroups. When school closures were threatened, into stormy meetings with parents and governors, when children were being bullied, exploited, or placed at risk, into their homes.

I also came to better understand the dangers that await the unwary in a city. Any city. My role, and that of my team of colleagues, included working directly with Greater Manchester Police, and other agencies, on initiatives to combat crime that impacted directly on young people. Initiatives to eliminate the carrying of knives and knife crime, mugging, drug use, membership of youth gangs and drug gangs in particular. I am especially proud of the fact that we were able to set up the first Police School Liaison Officers scheme in the country.

I came to see the city through the eyes of those who lived and worked there, many of them for generations, as well as through many who were new to the city as economic migrants, victims of war and ethnic cleansing.

Once I retired from that role, and had embarked on a new career as a crime fiction writer, it was inevitable that these experiences should influence the plotting, characterisation, and settings of my books.

As a reader I have always been drawn to writers who manage to capture the essence of the places in which their stories are set. When I plan a novel I visit every potential crime scene setting with a camera and voice recorder. I record how it looks, how it feels, even how it smells. Some of that I try to capture when I start to write. The majority of the feedback that I receive, especially from expats living in America, Canada and in Australia, is positive when it comes to the amount of detail I include about the city. A few find it a distraction. To those few I can only apologise,

The walks in this book are interspersed with extracts from relevant settings in one or more of the books. I have highlighted them so that if you wish you can simply skip them .

Finally, I have recommended some places to eat and drink along the way. These are ones that have proved consistently good value, and have stood the test of time. I have not been offered, or sought, any freebies or other inducements to make these recommendations, and the city is so blessed with alternative venues that you'll have plenty of other options.

I hope that you enjoy these walks. Even if you are familiar with the city, I hope that you discover something new along the way. If you arrive a stranger, I am certain and that you will leave as a friend, vowing to return.

Manchester

"A city that thinks a table is for dancing on."
Mark Radcliffe

'...AND
ON THE SIXTH DAY,
GOD CREATED
MANchester.'

Leo B Stanley – Afflecks Palace, and The Venue

'For a big City, Manchester is just small enough... 'We do
things differently here."
Tony Wilson

"I feel close to the rebelliousness and vigour of the youth here.
Perhaps time will separate us, but nobody can deny that here,
behind the windows of Manchester, there is an insane love of
football, of celebration, and of music.'
Eric Cantona.

"Manchester's got everything except a beach."
Ian Brown – Stone Roses

Walk 1
Around Deansgate

This is a circular walk around the main city centre thoroughfare of Deansgate, visiting Spinningfields, St John's Gardens, The Old Nag's Head, Manchester Central Library, The Town Hall, St Mary's Hidden Gem, The Ryland's Library, St Ann's Church, and The Royal Exchange.

Associated Titles: The Cleansing, The Head Case, A Fatal Intervention, A Venetian Moon.

Distance:

Total Distance:	3 kilometres/ 1.9 miles.
Total Walking Time:	45 Minutes

Allow at least the same amount of time again for exploration of the Town Hall, the John Rylands Library, The Central Library, and the Royal Exchange Theatre.

Terrain:
Pavements and pedestrianised streets. Flat, but with some uneven surfaces. Easy Walking.

Access issues:
Suitable for wheelchair users. There are ramps or lifts into the Town Hall, John Rylands Library, and Royal Exchange Theatre, and a lift alongside the steps into Hardman Square at the end of the walk.

Getting There:
By Car: Follow signs for the city centre, and then for Spinningfields. Spinningfields is adjacent to Deansgate, Manchester's main thoroughfare for pedestrians and road traffic. The most convenient parking can be found at 3 Hardman Street, Spinningfields, and 24

hour secure underground parking can be found just off Hardman Street by sat nav with the postcode: M3 3HF.

Hardman St can be accessed from Deansgate or off Quay Street onto Byrom St. Parking charges apply. NCP parking can also be found on New Quay St and Bridge St West for Spinningfields and The Avenue.

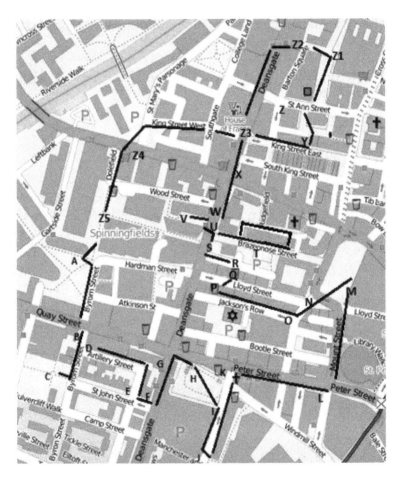

© OpenStreetMap contributors - opendatacommons.org

Start (A)   In Hardman Square, Spinningfields, the Financial Centre of the city.   Stand with your back to Pret A Manger, with Carluccio's Restaurant across to your right.   Set off in the direction of the Beetham Tower – a tall glass blade towering above and behind the South East corner of the square. After 100 yards join Byrom Street and continue forward to the junction with Quay Street. Turn right, and cross Quay Street at the traffic lights. Head up Quay Street with The Opera House on the opposite side to you, and turn first right into the continuation of Byrom Street. **(B)**. After 100 yards arrive, on your right, at the iron gates to **St John's Gardens**. This was the very first crime scene and deposition site in *The Cleansing*. Enter the gardens, and walk straight ahead to the cross. **(C).**

Extract 1.

"As he passed the stone cross, Caton glanced briefly at the inscription on its east face. He already knew what was written there: *St John's Church, which was taken down in 1931, was built on this site in 1769 by Edward Byrn, around the remains of more than 22,000 people.*

Plague, cholera and starvation had haunted the past of every city, and for too many they still afflicted the present. But mankind's capacity for evil seemed to Caton of a different order altogether. He recalled a poem by an anonymous local poet he had seen in the Manchester United trophy room.

As Satan was flying over Clayton for Hell
He was chained in the smoke, likewise the smell,
Quoth he: I'm not sure in what country I roam,
But I'm sure by the smell, I'm not far from home.

Caton shook his head, turned up the collar of his jacket and strode towards the west gate."

The Cleansing

In these gardens you will also find the grave and memorial stone to John Owens, founder of the Owens College that became

Manchester University. Now retrace your steps to the gate. Opposite you is St John's Street, where among the Georgian terraces, home to the law firms that service the nearby civil and criminal courts, are hidden the Chambers to which belonged Robert Thornton the unfortunate barrister featured in A Fatal Intervention. Turn left to retrace your steps along Byrom Street. After 50 yards turn first right into Artillery Street **(D)**. Note the blue plaque on the wall stating:

"In November 1745 Jacobite forces under Charles Edward Stuart – Bonnie Prince Charlie - used this site as a gun park."

At the far end of Artillery Street, as you turn right into Longworth Street, note the entrance to **Rafa's El Rincon.** This is the restaurant mentioned in a number of the books, and to which Caton brought Kate, among others. It is the oldest and most authentic tapas bar and restaurant in the North West, much frequented by premiership footballers, as evidenced by the framed shirts on the walls. Continue along Longworth Street, emerging after 60 yards into St John's Street. **(E).**

Turn left and walk up to Deansgate, the main thoroughfare through the city centre. Pause for a moment to look to your right. At the far end is the impressive, if incongruous, **Beetham Tower** housing the offices of Ying Zheng Xiong, the sinister Chief Executive of the Manchester and Shanghai Trading Corporation. It also houses the Hilton Hotel and the Cloud Bar from which you'll have magnificent 360 degree views across the city and the whole region. Opposite you, for the entire length of Deansgate down to the Beetham Tower are the red brick former offices and warehouses of the LNER Great Northern Railway. **(F).**

Turn left, and head down Deansgate to the lights at the junction with Peter Street. **(G).** Cross to your right at these lights and walk into the Great Northern Square. **(H).** The red and blue brick building facing you is the **Great Northern Warehouse**, a grade 2 listed building. This warehouse was constructed above the Manchester and Salford junction Canal so that goods could be lifted from the barges and transferred directly to the railway wagons above. The tunnels still remain, and were the setting for the dramatic conclusion to *A Fatal Intervention.*

"The exit from the chamber was into a tunnel the width of a small street, strewn with broken bricks and a century's accumulation of dust. He kept close to the left-hand side, trailing his hand along the dank wall to aid his balance. In less than a minute he found himself in another chamber, much larger than the first. The ceiling was high and vaulted. He heard a scurrying sound, and his heart skipped a beat. He lowered the torch and followed the sound. A rat the size of a domestic cat stopped and froze for a moment, caught in the centre of the beam. Its beady eyes seemed to glow. He could see the whiskers on its face twitching, slivers of silver. Then, as suddenly, it was gone."

A Fatal Intervention

Head diagonally ahead of you for the furthest corner of the square and the impressive block of glass and steel apartments – The Great Northern Tower. **(I).** Turn Right down Watson Street, past the champagne bar on your left, and continue for 90 yards to the entrance to the casino - **MANCH235TER**. The casino houses an exotic Chinese restaurant, and Celebrity Chef James Martin's Restaurant aptly named – James Martin Manchester. MANCH235TER is where Robert Thornton celebrated a disastrous New Year's Eve in A Fatal Intervention. Continue for a few yards to the end of the apartments on your left, **(J),** and then look up at the balconies perched above you. It was from one of these balconies that Robert Thornton saw the first indications of a crime scene beneath the brick arch ahead of you at the bottom of Watson Street.

"Perched on the end of the Great Northern Tower, his apartment faced south. Not best of outlooks during the day across the flat roof of the Great Northern Warehouse and the curve of the G-Mex exhibition centre – like a long round sliced loaf, it did at least catch the bulk of the day's sunlight. At night, however, there was a different kind of magic. He leant on the handrail and looked up at the night sky. This high up, despite the light pollution from the city, he was able to see a number of twinkling constellations.

Lowering his gaze, he could just make out the low dark mass of the Pennine hills at the south-eastern limit of his view, the red and white snakes of traffic on the Mancunian Way appearing and disappearing between the university buildings, and straight ahead, bisecting the night sky, the blue glass blade of the Beetham Tower. He could see people the size of ants in the Sky Bar of the Hilton Hotel. A wail of sirens troubled the gentle city hum. Blue lights were flashing in the tiny triangle of space where Watson Street and Great Bridgewater Street met. He watched and wondered, until the wind whipped up and an icy chill in the breeze forced him inside."

A Fatal Intervention

Retrace your steps to the Great Northern Square. On reaching the square continue straight ahead along Watson Street, and stop at the junction with Peter Street, **(K),** opposite the Grade 2 listed Baroque and Gothic style **Albert Hall.** This former Methodist Central Hall is now a stunning music venue that hosted the inaugural events of the 2013 Manchester International Festival.

Turn right and head up St Peter Street for 80 yards to the furthest corner of the colonnaded Radisson Hotel. This building was originally **The Free Trade Hall.** Erected on the site of the Peterloo Massacre (See plaque on the wall for details) this building oozes history. Built to celebrate the repeal of the Corn Laws it hosted many political meetings and rallies reflecting Manchester's Radical Liberal history. Charles Dickens, Disraeli, and Churchill all spoke here. As did Suffragettes Christabel Pankhurst and Annie Kenney whose ejection from the building, and arrest, marked the beginning of the Women's Social and Political Union's militant campaign for Women's Rights. It became Manchester's principle concert venue, and home of the Hallé orchestra. It also hosted pop and rock concerts. The most notable including Bob Dylan's first controversial electric guitar performance, Genesis, Pink Floyd, and in 1976 the concert at the Lesser Free Trade Hall by the Sex Pistols, attended by Caton, that marked the start of punk rock. Incidentally, they do a pretty good value afternoon tea here.

Continue up St Peter's Street to the corner of St Peter's Street and Mount Street where stands the famous **Midland Hotel, (L).** Two Michelin starred Simon Rogan – one of the country's most innovative and exciting chefs - is executive chef of the two restaurants here, dividing his time between The Midland, Claridges, and L'Enclume in Cartmel.

Cross St Peter's Street at the lights, and head down Mount Street with the iconic circular **Manchester Central Library** on your right hand side. This magnificent Grade 2 listed neo-classical building, inspired by the Pantheon in Rome, is the second largest public lending library in Britain. A £50 million make over was completed in February 2014, providing a vast, bright, airy learning hub fit for the 21st Century. The hundreds of thousands of books and and manuscripts – including a 12th-century hand written code of law originally compiled for the Roman Emperor Justinian – Codex Justinianus - and Shakespeare's Second Folio from 1632 - are still the heart of the library, but information technology is everywhere. Even in the cafe, where glass topped tables can be used like tablet computers to access resources while you drink your coffee, and scoff your Manchester fruit loaf. Young readers are treasured here, with a children's library based on Frances Hodgson Burnett's Secret Garden, and a gaming area stocked with Playstations and Xboxes.

After 150 yards you will reach Albert Square, and Alfred Waterhouse's wonderful Victorian **Gothic Manchester Town Hall. (M).** One of the most important Grade 1 listed buildings in the country, much used as a setting for films and TV, it is a must see venue. Apart from providing a dramatic climax to *The Cleansing*, it was also the headquarters to which I had regularly to report during my 18 years with the City Council. Visit the Great Hall with its murals by Ford Maddox Brown illustrating the history of the city, the Sculpture Hall that doubles as a cafe from Monday to Saturday, and the spectacular Mayor's Parlour, and the Banqueting Room. It is advisable to check in advance which rooms will be available.

Back out on the street step back and look up at the clock tower, and then at the turret to the right which has a flagpole. This was the place from which Caton attempted to negotiate a conclusion to the hostage situation in *The Cleansing*.

"Caton stepped cautiously onto the flat pavilion roof. One by one, the others followed him until all four were crouched with their backs to the vast stone chimney towering above them, masking them from the hostage and the hostage taker. The rifle officer and his buddy hunkered down in a huddle, lost in their own secret world."

The Cleansing

With your back to the Town Hall entrance head diagonally across the square to the left of the central statue of Oliver Heywood, to the West corner, at the junction of Lloyd Street and Southmill Street. **(N).** On your left is the Albert Square Chop House in the listed former Victorian Warehouse, and Thomas Worthington's memorial hall. Ahead of you is another iconic listed building with arguably the most impressive restaurant entrance. This is currently home to Red's BBQ Restaurant.

Tom's Tip: Both of these restaurants offer unpretentious food at sensible prices.

Take the left fork between these restaurants along Southmill Street. After 30 yards turn first left into Jackson's Row. **(0).**

The white stone building on the corner facing you is the former **Bootle Street Central Police Station** – which moved to the Town Hall Extension in Spring 2014. Head for 120 yards down

Jackson's Row towards Deansgate. Stand with your back to the Manchester Central Synagogue and look across at the **Old Nag's Head**, Caton's favourite watering hole, and home to his Reading Group – The Alternatives. This was formerly two pubs adjacent to each other. The Eighteenth Century hostelry was rebuilt in 1880, and the two pubs were merged in 1923, as evidenced by the plaques on the upper storey. It has remained largely unchanged since then. It has a small roof top terrace popular throughout the summer months.

"He turned into Jackson's Row. The freshly painted sign of The Old Nag's Head beckoned halfway up the narrow street, rising gently before him. Caton had much preferred the original sign with its wicked caricature, somewhere between the witch in Hansel and Gretel and a hooked-nose crone straight out of Dickens. He understood why it sat uncomfortably in a city committed to equality, but the sad and aged horse's head which had replaced it could never inspire the same affection, or reflect the true history of Manchester's past, except perhaps to represent a phase of safe, and edgeless, conformity.

Halfway up the adjoining Bootle Street there would be a line of police vans outside the garage entrance to the nick, preparing for the invasion of clubbers, stags and hens who had survived the previous two nights, and had the stamina for one more frantic round."

The Cleansing

Enter The Old Nag's Head, and walk through to the far side, and out into Lloyd Street. **(P)**. Across the street to your right you will see the small white frontage of **The Rising Sun. (Q).** Of a similar date to the Old Nag's Head this is another 'cut' pub, so called because they straddle two streets with entrances on both sides enabling punters to cut through from one street to the other. Were they designed this way so that if either the police or the wife came in through one side the customer could escape through the other? Or was it simply to maximise trade? You decide. These are two of the oldest traditional Mancunian city centre pubs that have eschewed the bar/gastropub genre and stuck to what they do best.

Enter The Rising Sun. On your way through to the far door note on the left the two wooden plaques, celebrating Manchester's unparalleled role in the Industrial Revolution, one of which reads:

"Manchester, First Industrial City. In 1780 it was always attracting the notice of outsiders as a centre of wealth creation and urban growth. After half a century of revolutionary change Manchester became the shock city of its age. It was the shock of the new which assaulted the senses and stimulated the imagination. The Industrial Revolution had arrived."

Turn left outside the Rising Sun, **(R).** and walk for 50 yards down to Deansgate. Turn right onto Deansgate. After 40 yards you will be outside Centurion House, with the RBS Bank Headquarters on the opposite side of the street, and Starbucks on your right. **(S).**

Starbucks is where the perpetrator in *Bluebell Hollow* waited for DS Stuart to emerge from the RBS offices. Continue ahead for 20 yards, stopping at the magnificent bronze of Chopin seated at a grand piano. This commemorates Chopin's visit to the city in 1848. Despite being gravely ill he insisted on giving a performance at the Gentlemen's Concert Hall on the corner of Peter Street and Lower Mosley Street. He died a year later. His decision to go ahead with the concert endeared him to the citizens of Manchester. On your right, immediately beyond the statue, is the long broad avenue of Brasenose Street. If you step 50 yards up this street you will be able to see another stunning bronze **statue of Abraham Lincoln. (T).**

This statue was destined to stand outside the Houses of Parliament, but the worthies of Manchester argued that this city had an unrivalled claim because of the heroic sacrifices that Lancashire cotton workers had made in support of the abolition of slavery despite the hardship caused by the Southern State's boycott of the cotton exports to Britain. Around the base of the statue are engraved copies of letters from Abraham Lincoln, including this one.

"To the working people of Manchester 19th January 1863. I know and deeply deplore the sufferings which the working people of Manchester and in all Europe are called to endure in this crisis. It has been often and studiously represented that the attempt to overthrow this Government which was built on the foundation of human rights, and to substitute for it one which should rest exclusively on the basis of slavery, was likely to obtain the favour of Europe. Through the action of disloyal citizens the working people of Europe have been subjected to a severe trial for the purpose of forcing their sanction to that attempt. Under these circumstances I cannot but regard your decisive utterances upon the question as an instance of sublime Christian heroism which has not been surpassed in any age or in any country. It is indeed an energetic and re-inspiring assurance of the inherent truth and of the ultimate and universal triumph of justice, humanity and freedom. I hail this interchange of sentiments therefore, as an augury that whatever else may happen, whatever misfortune may befall your country or my own, the peace and friendship which now exists between the two nations will be as it shall be my desire to make them, perpetual."

At this point those unable to negotiate three sets of three stone steps should return to Deansgate and continue from point **U** below.

Walkers should continue past the statue, up Brasenose Street, for 38 yards, and then turn left up the steps that lead through a broad passage into Mulberry Street. Immediately opposite you is the Church of St Mary, affectionately known by Mancunians as **The Hidden Gem**. Tom and Kate were married here in *Backwash*.

"He could have done without his team slipping white Tyvek protective all in ones over their wedding outfits, and holding batons out to create a triumphal arch as they left the church, but in all other respects the wedding had exceeded their expectations."

Backwash

A spiritual oasis in the heart of the city for people of all faiths, and none, St Mary's was the first Post Reformation Roman

Catholic Church in Manchester, and celebrated its bi-centenary in 1994. Rebuilt in the 1930s it has some stunning features, including the reredos of white Caen stone above the high altar, a side altar of marble and Caen stone dominated by a life size pieta, the stained glass window representing the Magnificat, and the brilliant and inspirational Fourteen Stations of The Cross, painted by the Royal Academician, Norman Adams who considers them to be the greatest works of his life. It is worth the detour just to see these paintings.

Turn right out of the church, and head down Mulberry Street for 95 yards, turning left at the bottom, and back out onto Brasenose Street. Now turn right back down to Deansgate. **(U).** Now continue to the first set of lights, and cross to the impressive and unmistakeable red sandstone **John Rylands Library,** widely regarded as one of the most beautiful libraries in the world, and on the list of *Visit England Top 101 things to do before you go abroad.* Head down by the side of the Library to the entrance, and into the cafe. **(V).** I suggest that you at least visit the Rylands Gallery on the first floor and above all, on the third floor, the **Historic Reading Room**, featured in several of the books, including *Bluebell Hollow.*

"His sense of panic rose as he moved from floor to floor, racing down the huge stone spiral staircase, searching the dark and gloomy rooms on either side. Close to despair, he entered the Historic Reading Room.
She was standing with her back towards him, beneath the delicate arching tracery of the Cumbrian granite roof. She was staring up at the white marble statue of Enriquetta Rowlands, the benefactor of this library, surrounded by the largest collection of rare books and manuscripts in Britain. He touched her gently on the shoulder, half expecting it to be someone else. It startled her from her reverie."

Bluebell Hollow.

Now head back up towards Deansgate, passing on your right the small glass entrance to *Australasia* - an excellent Asian fusion restaurant located underground, in the former print room of the Manchester Guardian and Manchester Evening News.

Kate's Tip: Australasia offers great deals on tapas style lunches.

Back on Deansgate, **(W)**, turn left and cross immediately at the traffic lights, and turn left on the opposite side. After 50 yards cross John Dalton Street, **(X)**. You are now standing outside *Katsouris* Caton's favourite cafe and delicatessen for breakfast and brunch. Even if you don't feel hungry you might want to pop inside and see the amazing deli counter, hot carvery, and salad bar. Continue north along Deansgate.

(Y). Turn second right into pedestrianised King Street East. Cross the aptly named Police Street, and after 50 yards turn left into the small arcaded passageway marked by three blue metal bollards. This typical Victorian Mancunian passage – formerly medieval - leads to St Ann's Square. Facing you is the Georgian period **Church of St Ann.** Turn left, and then right into the square, passing the flower seller from whom Caton gets his flowers for Kate. Enter the church. **(Z)**.

This church – the only remaining Protestant church in the city centre - had two miraculous escapes. The first during the blitz of Manchester during the Second World War when an incendiary bomb that plummeted through the roof into the church failed to ignite. The incendiary has been defused, and is kept in the church safe, but can be viewed on request. The second, was that the church escaped with only minor damage to some of the windows from the IRA bomb that devastated much of the area. One of the windows that was repaired in situ after the blast is the first one on your left. It depicts King Solomon and has an inscription to the *First Architect of The Universe.* Fans of Dan Brown's books will recognise this as a Masonic reference, and may spot the numerous Freemasonry symbols in the stained glass including compass and square, twin pillars, pyramid, and beehive. There are a number of other windows with such symbols as well as symbols for the Kabbalah, the body of Jewish mysticism adopted by numerous Hollywood celebrities.

On leaving St Ann's Church head directly ahead through the square until you reach, on your right, the **Royal Exchange Theatre. (Z1).** Formerly the Cotton Exchange, this building was once twice the size you see now, and was the largest indoor space in Europe. It is now home to Britain's largest theatre in the round, seating 700 people, and is our foremost Northern theatre. As you enter prepare to be astounded by the sumptuous Classical interior, as well as the seven sided glass and steel module that stands in the centre, suspended from the marble pillars like some alien space craft. No seat in this unique theatre is more than nine metres from the centre of the stage. The intimacy that this creates for actors and audience alike provides an unrivalled theatrical experience. More so if you happen, like Caton and his creator, to prefer the banquettes than bring you within a few feet of the actors.

Having recovered from a direct hit during the Blitz of 1940, the Royal Exchange was extensively damaged on 15 June 1996 by the IRA bomb detonated less than 50 yards away. Opened by Sir Laurence Olivier two years, and £32 million later, it emerged with a second performance space, restaurant, bars, workshop and craft shop. In 1999 it was awarded Theatre of The Year in the Barclays Theatre Awards. The roll call of world famous actors who have, and continue to appear here, is too extensive to list..

Leave the Royal Exchange and head diagonally left across the pedestrian precinct, turn first right into Barton Square, and head for the Victorian glass and steel **Barton Arcade** immediately ahead of you. **(Z2).** Enter the arcade, and pass through to the far side exiting onto Deansgate. Turn left and walk to the first set of traffic lights opposite Bella Italia. Cross here, and then turn left, across St Mary's Street, heading back down Deansgate passing on your right the House of Fraser, still known affectionately by its original name Kendals.

Kate's Tip: When you've finished the walk this is a great place for retail therapy. Plus there's a champagne bar, and Cicchetti restaurant and bar. Girls, It's a no brainer!

At the far end of Kendals turn right into King Street West. **(Z3).** Walk ahead. On your right you will pass *San Carlo Cicchetti,* a delightful restaurant that offers a new take on the Venetian dishes enjoyed by Donna Leon's Commissario Brunetti, as well as Caton and Kate. Small plate dishes, a sort of Italian Tapas, to share or eat alone, with a glass of wine, or beer. Full English breakfasts too. On the opposite side of road is *San Carlo*, the flagship restaurant of this chain in the city, featured in *A Venetian Moon*. Expect to see chauffeured limousines and high-end sports cars parked here, and paparazzi lingering in the shadows.

" San Carlo was packed. They had five minutes to wait while their table was prepared. They waited by the bar.

Umberto Bonifati was amazed.

'Una serata di Lunedi!' he exclaimed. 'All these people, on a Monday?'

'It's like this every evening,' Caton told him. 'Welcome to Manchester, Umberto.'

He pointed to a table away on the right-hand side to which Caterina Volpe's eyes had already been drawn.

'That's half the Man United team,' he said. 'And over there, for good measure…' He pointed to the opposite side of the room. '…are a couple of Man City players with their partners. Monday is a popular night for footballers. One of the few they can let their hair down.'

'They always come here?'

'Here, and San Rocco, and Puccini's in Swinton. And any time now they'll be trying out George's Place – Ryan Giggs' new restaurant in Worsley. I told you, you're spoilt for choice.'

The Italian looked doubtful.

'I hope they have good taste,' he said. 'In my experience the best food come in trattoria e osteria.'

Caton could see the padrone coming to tell them that their table was ready.

'You're about to find out,' he said.

Caterina Volpe chose the seat that gave her the best view of the United players, and tutted when her boss chose the seat immediately opposite her, partly obscuring her view. Caton suspected that Umberto had done it on purpose.

From the outset there appeared to be an unspoken agreement not to talk about the case. Umberto in particular would have had difficulty finding the time to talk about anything, so engrossed was he in his Marinata Di Verdure Alla Griglia – chargrilled aubergines, courgettes and peppers marinated in fresh mint, extra virgin olive oil, garlic and chilli, served with buffalo mozzarella and parsley, followed by a Venetian favourite, Fegato Di Vitello Alla Veneziana – calf's liver with polenta, in an onion and Madeira wine sauce.

Caterina chose a single dish of Risotto Agli Scampi, made with a white wine, cream and tomato sauce, which took her as long to eat as did Umberto his first two courses.

Caton started with scallops in white wine and garlic on sautéed spinach, and followed it with one of his favourites, Garganelli Salsiccia e Porcini – egg pasta with spicy sausage, porcini mushroom and a light tomato sauce...

...She passed on dessert. Umberto and Caton shared a selection of Italian cheeses.

'Well?' said Caton as they relaxed with a coffee.

'Not bad,' said Umberto.

Caterina Volpe shrugged, and waggled her head from side to side.

Caton judged that an outright success. About as good as it got. Neither of them was going to admit it, but compared with the food that most of the restaurants in Venice served up this had been exceptional. With twenty-seven chefs in the kitchen, all Italian trained and all handpicked, it was hardly surprising. "

A Venetian Moon

Tom's Tip: If you're tempted to lunch or dine at San Carlo, and why wouldn't you be, it's always best to book ahead.

Cross over, and continue on down King Street West, turning left at the end into the small square named Motor Street. Continue to the lights on your left. Cross Bridge Street at the lights opposite the Central Masonic Lodge and turn right. 10

yards on your left is The Avenue North. **(Z4).** Before turning into The Avenue pause to look ahead of you at the Waitrose Express on the corner.

On the 15th of June 1996 when the IRA bomb exploded I was sitting in my car 1,500 yards from the epicentre. My senior inspector colleague Mick Molloy, having been evacuated from Albert Square by the police, was also in his car, with the windows down, outside Martins Newsagents, now the Waitrose store. The blast from the bomb travelled down St Mary's Gate to your right, which acted like a super wind tunnel, passed through the car, and blew a woman who happened to be walking by, into and through the plate glass window of the shop. Thankfully, neither she, Mick, nor his passengers were badly injured. On a windy day it is still possible to imagine that blast sweeping through these streets.

Turn left into The Avenue North. Before entering the Avenue look up at Tower 12 – the building on your right. This is contains the Lounge and Restaurant of Manchester House, celebrity chef Aiden Byrne's fine dining restaurant.

Continue ahead into the Avenue North, past the high end retail shops. Pause at the end of the Avenue, and look up at the glass and redbrick office block to your left, immediately above the Gucci store, and to the right of the Oast House restaurant and bar. These offices, know as Crown Square, were originally the Manchester Education offices, my home base. From the last of the offices I occupied in this building I was able to look directly down at the spot where you are standing, and out across Crown Square at the Crown Courts where criminal justice was, and still is, dispensed. In fact my first act as District Inspector, on my first day in post, was to cross the square and take a lift up to the cells on the roof of the building on the end of the Crown Courts, to suspend a teacher who had been accused of dealing drugs from the school minibus during a school camp. He was eventually found not guilty, but subsequently dismissed for other misdemeanours.

Continue ahead past the two olive trees in blue slate planters, alongside the Oast House. At the end of the office block, **(Z5)**, turn left, and continue straight ahead, up the steps and into Hardman Square where you began.

Walk 2
Around the Cathedral Gardens

Associated Titles: The Head Case

This is a circular walk around the most historic medieval part of the city centre, visiting The Cathedral and Collegiate Church of St Mary, St Denys and St George, Chetham's Library, The Corn Exchange and, a touch of the modern, The National Museum of Football. And at the end the promise of exceptional retail therapy for those so inclined.

This is a fascinating area that, aside from its medieval history, was at the heart of the devastation caused by the Provisional IRA Bombing on 15th June 1996 - the largest bomb ever detonated on mainland Britain. The subsequent redevelopment of this area of the city marked one of the most successful and ambitious urban redevelopments in modern times

It is also less than a stone's throw from Kate's favourite city retail therapy destinations, Harvey Nichols, Selfridges, M&S, TK Maxx, St Ann's Square, and the Arndale Centre.

There is a plethora of restaurants, bars and cafes around Exchange Square, the Corn Exchange, and inside The Print Works.

Note: Chetham's Library is not open to visitors at weekends.

Distance:

Total Distance:	1,000 yards - ¾ of a mile.
Total Walking Time:	20 minutes

Allow at least 2 hours for exploration of the visitor attractions and, if so minded, at least another 2 hours for retail therapy. And then there's Lunch!

Terrain: Pavements and pedestrianised streets. Easy Walking.

Access issues:
Suitable for accompanied wheelchair, and mobility scooter access. Access is not a issue at either The Cathedral, or The National Football Museum. At Chetham's Library wheelchair users and others unable to manage stairs have access to the collections by the use of ground floor study rooms, but are unfortunately unable to visit the historic first floor library. Please contact the Library in advance with details of your requirements. Access to The Corn Exchange is via a ramp at the main entrance on Exchange Square. Inside the Corn Exchange is a glass lift to all floors.

Getting There.
By car
Travelling from the North and East on the M62 - leave at junction 17 (A56) Follow for approximately 5 miles. When you pass MEN Arena the Cathedral is under the bridge on the left.

Travelling from the South and West M6 - M62 - M602, follow the signs for the City Centre. On arriving at Deansgate turn left along Deansgate and continue to the end. The Cathedral is on the right, and car park signs abound.

Parking
Ample parking is available at the NCP at Old Exchange Station approach and in the MEN Arena which are both in the immediate vicinity of Manchester Cathedral. There is a multi-storey car park at the nearby Manchester Evening News Arena, the entrance is on Trinity Way M3 1LE Charges from 6-24hrs £18 on weekdays, but at Weekends from 0.900 – 17.00 it is only £2 [Correct at 5/02/2014]

By Train
Victoria Station is right by the start of the walk. Metrolink trams and the free Metro Shuttle buses all call here. See link below for Transport for Greater Manchester.

Link: http://www.tfgm.com/Pages/default.aspx

Start (A) At the entrance to Victoria Station. Cross the road at the lights. turn left along Hunts Bank, and follow it around to the right onto Todd Street. After 85 yards at point **[B]**, turn right onto the paved path that leads to **Chetham's Library**. The grassed area is on your left-hand side. After 70 yards arrive at the entrance to Chetham's Library.

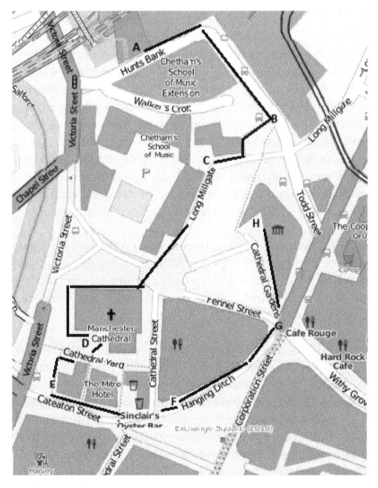

Entrance is free, although a much needed donation would be appreciated. The Library is open to visitors Monday to Friday 9.00-12.30 a.m. and 1.30-4.30 p.m. If you wish to read any of the books or manuscripts you will need to make an appointment. Ring 0161 834 7961, or email: librarian@chethams.org.uk

Founded in 1653 Chet's, as it is affectionately known, is the oldest functioning public library fully and freely accessible to the public in the English-speaking world. [Biblioteca Malatestiana in Cesena, Italy, is the oldest such library in the modern world]. The Chetham's Library's entire collection of books and rare manuscripts have been designated as of international importance, and you can search the catalogue online before visiting in person. The building in which it is housed predates the library, having been built in 1491 to accommodate a college of priests. It is worth a visit simply to see these rooms and soak up the atmosphere. Karl Marx, and Friedrich Engels met and studied together in the library during the period when they were formulating their political theory that would emerge in Karl Marx's Communist Manifesto. The desk and chair remain today exactly as they were when Engels occupied them.

Leaving Chetham's Library, turn right with the grassed area on your left, and head down Long Millgate alongside Chetham's School of Music. After 200 yards turn right to skirt the West side of the Cathedral. After 80 yards reach the entrance to **Manchester Cathedral. [D]**

This is regarded as one of the most impressive late medieval collegiate churches in England. Following the destruction by the Danes of a 7th Century Saxon church a new church - the first St Mary's Church - was built on or near this spot in 923. Standing on a small sandstone bluff, in a defensive position beside the Manor Hall – now Chetham's Library – it was surrounded by the River Irwell, the River Irk, and an ancient watercourse known as the Hanging Ditch. A bridge – The Hanging Bridge – linked both Church and manor to the township. In 1215 this church was replaced by a larger one, and from 1421 onwards it was gradually transformed into the impressive collegiate church of St Mary, St Denys and St George that you see today. Enter the Cathedral, and wander at your leisure. The volunteer Guides are really helpful, and free. Use this website to plan your visit:

Link: http://www.manchestercathedral.org/a-good-day-out

Make sure that at the very least you visit the Chapel of the Duke of Lancaster Regiment with its magnificent flame window. The entire exterior wall and much of the rest of this chapel were destroyed by a bomb in the 1940 Blitz. The Fire Window has therefore both a spiritual and a historical meaning. See if you can find the beige stone memorial tablet to the Lever children on the West wall just outside the chapel, referred to in *The Head Case.*

> *Here d'yd their Parents' hopes and feares'.*
> *Once all their joy, now all their teares',*
> *They'r now past hope, past feare, or paine,*
> *It were a Sinne to wish them here againe.*

The Head Case

Also be sure to inspect the beautiful and intricately carved rood screen, and visit the choir to see the set of misericords on the underside of the choir stall seats.

"The Cathedral was filling rapidly. Only the front section of this, the widest nave in England, had been set out with chairs in order to achieve the illusion of large numbers. Nevertheless, the turnout was impressive.   Caton and Holmes chose seats at the back, in the north aisle, with a clear view of the flame red window of the military chapel.

The cathedral was as imposing as Caton remembered it from the first time he had come here as a member of the choir of Manchester Grammar School. The graceful gothic arches soared skyward, above the magnificent mediaeval quire screen, towards the intricately carved roof of the nave, punctuated by golden sunburst bosses. He had always thought that the carvings on the misericords of Reynold the Fox, and the woman scolding her husband for breaking a pot, were a testimony to the fact that Mancunian humour had its roots in history."

The Head Case

The Dean's choir stall on the right as you enter the choir was occupied in 1596 by Dr John Dee, a genuine spy, who signed his letters to the Queen, 007, so that she would know that they were for her eyes only. Ian Fleming happily borrowed the cipher for his own spy – James Bond. Dee was sent here by Queen Elizabeth as Warden of Christ's College to spy on the college of priests, one of whom was keeping a Beer House, and another of whom was selling church property for his own advantage.

Leave the Cathedral and enter the *Propertea Cafe* in Hanging Bridge Chambers immediately ahead of you. This is also the Cathedral Centre Cafe, and gives access to the Library and Bookshop

Kate's Tip: *Propertea* is a perfect place for a tea or coffee break. Scrumptious cakes and scones!

At the far end of the cafe the doors lead onto a walkway from which you will be able to view the remains of the eponymous **Hanging Bridge**, even when the bookshop is closed.

" 'Where do you want to meet me? The Mitre, The Crown and Anchor, The Old Wellington, or Sinclair's Oyster Bar?'

Caton had to smile. 'It's a Memorial Service, Gordon, not a pub crawl. And we're on duty, remember?'

'It's not as though it's a funeral though, is it?'

'Wait for me in the Hanging Bridge, Gordon. Get yourself a coffee. I'll be about ten minutes.' "

"Holmes was sitting at a table for two, in the basement of the Cathedral Shop in Cateaton Street, looking down on the exposed section of the original medieval stone bridge from which the café drew its name. The bridge used to link this part of the city with the Cathedral, across the ditch in which the rivers Irwell and Irk met. Whether people were ever hung here, Caton's Local History studies at MGS group had never revealed. Holmes finished his drink, and they climbed back up to the shop, turned right outside, and started the short journey to the Cathedral entrance."

The Head Case

Leave either the Bookshop or Propertea, and make you way onto Cateaton Street at point **[E]**. Turn left, and continue left along Cateaton Street, past two excellent Victorian Pubs - the Crown and Anchor, and The Mitre, and pause in Shambles Square, outside **The Old Wellington,** and **Sinclair's Oyster House**.

These are both Grade 1 listed buildings. The Old Wellington, a scheduled Ancient Monument, is the oldest remaining property of its type in the city, the rest of the Shambles having been destroyed during the Blitz of December 22nd-24th 1940. Built in 1552, it was a drapers and a bank before in became a licensed public house in 1830. The upper storey housed an optical and mathematical instruments maker, and then a fishing tackle shop. The entire building has been moved twice; in the late 1970s it was moved intact into the Arndale Centre, and following the 1996 IRA bomb it was deconstructeded, and rebuilt 300 yards away in its current position, close to the original Shambles and Marketplace. Sinclair's Oyster Bar began life as a John Shaw's Punch House in the 18th Century. In 1796 it became known as Sinclair's, and in 1845 the name changed to reflect the fact that oysters had been added to the menu, where they remain to this day.

Continue left along Hanging Ditch, past the **Corn Exchange**. **[F]**. This Grade 2 listed Edwardian building, built in 1837 as the Corn and Produce Exchange, was restored following the 1996 IRA bombing, and is currently undergoing a £15m redevelopment to create a bustling cosmopolitan indoor eating venue, housing a dozen or so independent restaurants and retail food outlets. This is due for completion by the end of 2014. Worth a visit for the architecture alone, those with mobility issues will need to continue for another 50 yards to arrive at the main entrance where there is a ramp.

Leave the Corn Exchange and turn left along Hanging Ditch to arrive at the junction of Corporation Street, Fennel Street, and Withy Grove. **[G]**. Look back down Corporation Street to your right. You may just be able to make out – 200 yards away – a **red post box**, beneath the glass walkway between Marks and Spencer and The Arndale. This marks the spot where the Provisional IRA Bomb exploded on 15th June 1996. Two hundred and twelve people were injured, and the cost of reconstruction had reached £1.1 billion by 2014. This was the the third IRA bombing of the city. In 1991 firebombs exploded in the Arndale Centre. In 1992 two bombs exploded; one close to the Cathedral, the other in Parsonage Gardens just off Deansgate. Sixty Five people were injured. The indomitable Mancunian spirit shrugged off each of these attacks – as it did the World War 2 Blitz - and no one can deny the physical improvements that the resultant bold and imaginative redevelopments have brought.

Cross Fennel Street and head up Cathedral Gardens alongside the distinctive finlike shape of the impressive **Urbis** building. After 100 yards arrive at the entrance to the **National Museum of Football**. Entry is free, and fascinating for adults and children alike – male and female – whether interested in football or not. There are charges for a few of the interactive extras, but these are well worth the money.

Kate's Tip: the Museum Cafe is less crowded than most others in the vicinity, ideal for light bites, and has excellent home baked pies in a pot.

Exit the Museum, turn right around the museum shop, and continue down the pedestrianised ramp to arrive back at Hunts bank. **[B]** Turn left here along Hunts bank for 85 yards to arrive back at **Victoria Station. [A]**.

Alternatively, head back to Exchange Square from where the world is Kate Caton's retail oyster. Then again, you could pop into Sinclair's Oyster House where you may just come across

DCI Caton and DI Gordon Holmes sharing a dozen or so of the real thing washed down with a beer or a glass of wine. Or you could try any one of the scores of excellent restaurants in the vicinity.

Kate's Tip: Hungry or thirsty? From the same San Carlo chain, try the San Carlo bottega, or the elegant Farmacia Del Dolce restaurant, cocktail and champagne bar, both in Selfridges.

Walk 3
Chinatown and the Gay Village

Associated Titles: The Cleansing, & The Tiger's Cave

About The Walk:

These two fascinating districts of the city, despite their close proximity, could not be more different. Each has its strong and thriving community, as well as being a magnet for other city dwellers and tourists from around the globe. This walk is easily accomplished in a leisurely couple of hours, including time out to visit Manchester City Art Gallery, and the Portico Library, and to explore the Chinese supermarkets. You may consider having breakfast in the Gay Village, and lunch or dinner in Chinatown. If Asian food isn't your thing, for lunch there is always the restaurant in the brilliant Manchester City Art Gallery, or home cooking in the unique and fascinating Portico Library. You may prefer to wander around each of these districts in a haphazard manner, exploring the side streets, and being constantly surprised by their delights and their diversity.

Getting There:

By Car: There are a number of car parks in and around the Gay Village and Chinatown itself. Check on Parkopedia.com, but be aware that they fill up quickly at peak times. The largest and most central is the Chorlton Street/Sackville Street NCP multi-storey. Sackville Street, Manchester M1 3NL

By Bus.

From Piccadilly Station, Oxford Rd Station, or close to Victoria Station, jump on either the Orange Route 1, or Purple Route 3 Free Metro Shuttle bus. Ask for The Gay Village stop closest to Canal Street and Sackville Gardens. Note, the Purple Route 3 does not run on Sundays or public holidays.

By Train. depending on your direction of travel, travel to any one of the city's mainline stations. There you will be able to transfer to a Metrolink tram. Check the routes, and alight at the Piccadilly Gardens, or St Peter's Square stops, both approximately 400 yards from the start of the walk. Better still – use the Free Metro Shuttle Bus Routes 1 or [See above]. From Oxford Road Station it is a 500 yard walk along Whitworth Street to the Gay Village.

Access Issues:
The **Portico Library:** Unfortunately the physical constraints of this historic building, specifically the steep narrow staircase, prevent access for wheelchair users. **The Gay Village and Chinatown:** Some, but not all of the venues listed such a restaurants, cafes, and bakeries, can only be accessed by stone steps.

Map 1. The First Section of the Walk - The Gay Village.

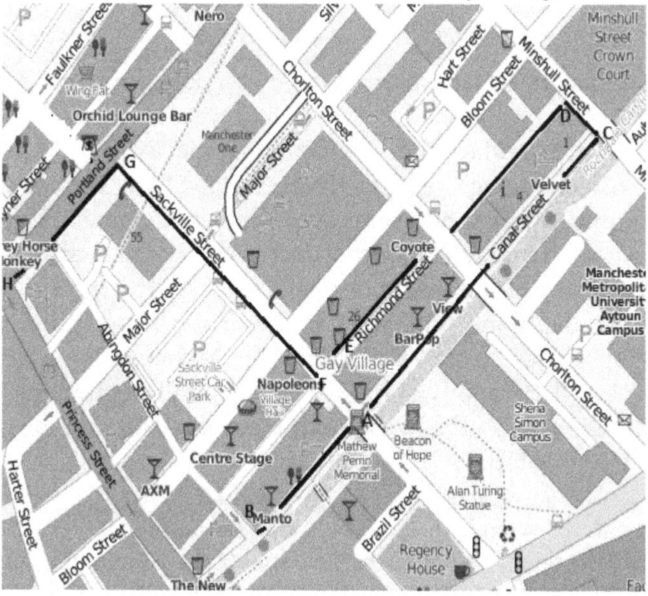

Map 2. Overview

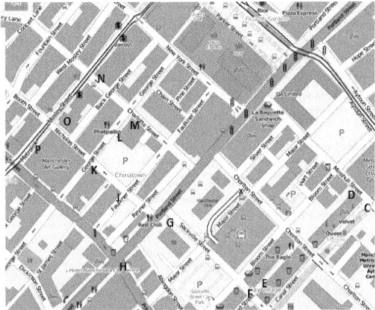

© OpenStreetMap contributors - opendatacommons.org

Start on the bridge at the junction of Sackville Street and Canal Street, facing the Rem Hotel and bar **[A]**. Formerly the Rembrandt, this bar hotel was one of the first to open following the Sexual Offences Act 1967 that decriminalised sexual relations in private between consenting men over 21. The owners were instrumental, along with the owners of the New Union pub, and Napoleon's, in the evolution of the Manchester Gay Pride Festival and Parade which grew, from small beginnings as a jumble sale outside the Rembrandt Hotel in 1990, into the huge event that it is today.

'The Rem? What is that, a cyber café?' Caton asked.

The two sergeants laughed. 'No, sir, it's the Rembrandt, one of the original bars in the Village. It's on the corner of Sackville Street and Canal Street; you must have passed it on your way to meet me.'

'I know where it is. I was a regular visitor at weekends, together with the heavy mob. I hope it's improved.'

'The Rembrandt never was a problem,' said DS Stuart, 'just the lunatic fringe that hung around the edge of the Village looking to cause trouble. Right now it's really popular, and as safe as any of the bars. In summer it opens right onto the canal; it really buzzes.' ...

The Cleansing

Turn left and walk down Canal Street for 60 yards, and stop outside Manto Bar. On your left is the Eden, the floating restaurant that features in The Cleansing.

" They waited for the stream of traffic down Princess Street to pass.

'You'd be surprised,' she said. 'Most of the new bars are straight, but lesbian and gay friendly, and there are nights when almost half of the people in the Village are straight; mainly groups and couples.'

She stopped opposite the Manto Bar and turned to face the canal, where a pretty green and white wooden bridge led across to the far bank.

Eden turned out to be a large red-brick converted mill. A black fire escape snaked up the frontage, giving access to an art gallery on the first floor, and safe exit from the floors above. The main restaurant bar appeared to be on the ground floor, and in the cellar. Moored alongside, a large open-topped barge set out with tables and chairs, and sporting a white sailcloth awning, was already beginning to fill up with early evening customers. An earnest young man in his late twenties waved up at them. "

Retrace your steps up Canal Street, past The REM to the end of the street. Take care crossing Chorlton Street on the way. Immediately opposite you at the end of Canal Street [C], is the imposing facade of, Thomas Worthington's European Gothic Minshull Street Crown Courts. Turn left, and stop outside the main entrance on the corner of Richmond Street. [D] There are some similarities to his designs for the Town Hall which lost out to those of Alfred Waterhouse. Both architects were devotees of Ruskin's passion for Venetian Gothic which you will find all over the city. Here, in the Crown Courts, Worthington has gone overboard with Gothic embellishments – in particular the strange and fierce beasts around the arches of the main doors, the gargoyles high up on the tower and campanile, and the owls standing guard on the gable finials. Pity the accused as they arrive for day one of their trial. But then again, maybe not, unless of course they are innocent.

Turn left down Richmond Street for 200 yards, re-crossing Chorlton Street as you go. Stop outside the Molly House on your left-hand side. **[E].** The name of this bar that reminds us that the streets around Canal Street were a notorious Red Light District in the long period between the decline of the factories and warehouses and the emergence of the vibrant bars, restaurants, and creative design offices that inhabit it today. If you arrive here from 12 pm onwards step inside and you'll find out why it was rated on Trip Advisor as the third best visitor attraction after the Royal Exchange and The Lowry. Aside from the tasty brunch and tapas menu, and the speciality teas and coffees, it oozes with class, eccentricity, and charm. There are books to borrow, and a wide range of national and international newspapers to read in the warm ambience of the bordello, the tea room, and the bar. There's even a red lit verandah with wine barrels for tables. Continue to the junction with Sackville Street, 20 yards, and turn right. **[F].** Continue ahead for 186 yards to reach Portland Street. **[G].**

Turn right and immediately cross at the lights. Turn left, cross Nicholas Street, and continue for 100 yards passing, on your right, the Circus Tavern. Rating itself as having the smallest bar in Europe – it's just two feet wide – Circus Tavern was originally a butcher's shop before becoming an ale house in the 1790. Its name is reputed to come from the period during which is was a favourite haunt of the entertainers from the permanent circuses that stood in this part of the city. Continue ahead to reach The Old Monkey Pub on the corner of Portland Street and Princess Street. **[H].** Turn right. Continue for 60 yards, and then pause opposite the red banners on the opposite side of the Street proclaiming YANG SING.

Founded in 1977 by the renowned Yeung family, the Yang Sing was one of the first and best restaurants established in Manchester's Chinatown in modern times. Housed in a beautiful grade 2 listed building it offers a modern twist on traditional high quality Cantonese cuisine. In 2012 it was deservedly listed among the Sunday Times top 10 restaurants in the North West. Certainly it is Kate's favourite.

Map 3. Chinatown

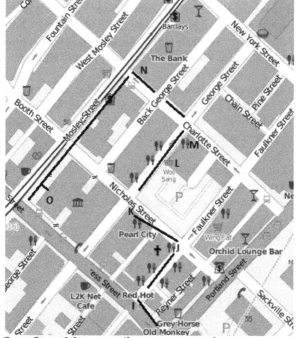

© OpenStreetMap contributors - opendatacommons.org

"The taxi dropped them at the corner of Charlotte Street and Portland Street. Caton paid the driver, and stepped back onto the pavement. Behind them lay Chinatown, ahead was the start of the Gay Village.

'OK,' he said. 'That narrows it down. We're talking Mediterranean, Asian Fusion, Japanese, Chinese, Indian, Thai, Vietnamese, or Italian. Probably not Indian, because then we'd be in Rusholme.'

Kate grabbed his arm, and slipped her own around it. 'You're so clever, Tom Caton. I'm amazed you never considered becoming a detective?' She whirled him round, and started off down Charlotte Street.

Caton began to check off the possibilities. There were three restaurants here that he had previously brought her to for lunch. There was another new buffet style one that he knew she rated for the same purpose. But for dinner, there were only three that had become firm joint favourites. As they crossed the junction with Faulkner Street he glanced West at the Imperial Arch, gleaming red, gold, and green in the reflected light. She led him left into George Street towards two strong contenders; *Pacific* with its Chinese and Thai cuisine each on separate floors; and his personal favourite, the *Little Yang Sing*. Kate watched his face as they sailed past...

...'Great choice.' Caton told her. 'Even better than the last time I was here.' He lifted a plump piece of braised duckling from the spicy yellow and black bean casserole. 'I like the way they've refurbished it too. I'm surprised they didn't do this after it was rebuilt following the fire.'

'I don't think modern 1930s Shanghai style décor was the rage then.' Kate replied, using her chopsticks to deftly wrap a whirl of Chinese greens around a succulent piece of monkfish fillet."

The Tiger's Cave

Now turn right into Faulkner Street. [I].   You are entering the heart of the second largest Chinatown in the Britain, and the third largest in Europe. Expanding rapidly from the 1970s onwards it is now the main financial, cultural, social, and educational hub for Chinese origin families in the North of England, serving a population of over 20,000 people of Chinese heritage, and a further 10,000 or more students at the city's universities and colleges. It is also famous throughout the region for its diverse Chinese and South East Asian restaurants, bakeries, and supermarkets. Not forgetting the Chinese New Year celebrations that attract many thousands of visitors to the city every year.

This bottom section of Faulkner Street, tiny though it is, is a typical cross section of Chinatown, with it's regional Chinese, Thai, and Japanese restaurants, a bookies, a hairdressers, a supermarket, a sweet shop, a bakery and cafe, Western Union, and the offices of Manchester Chinese Cultural Services. At the end of the street, stop facing the glorious paifang, or Imperial Arch. [J].

"Chinatown was so much smaller than he had expected; a rectangle of streets, five blocks by three, teeming with restaurants, supermarkets, banks, bakeries, and herbalists. He had taken the precaution of coming in the evening to lessen the risk of discovery, only to find this the most colourful, brightly lit, part of the city. The biggest surprise came as he turned the corner into Faulkner Street, and was confronted by the Imperial Chinese Archway.

He stood transfixed, staring up at the magnificent structure towering above the narrow street. A small group of tourists, fellow countrymen and women, appeared as if from nowhere, pushing forward, surrounding him as they pressed to take their photographs. Their guide stood to one side, her closed umbrella raised above her head; one moment a rallying point, the next a pointer.

'This is the only true Imperial Chinese Archway in the whole of Europe,' she began. 'It is even more magnificent than the more famous arch in San Francisco, America. This unique Ching Dynasty Arch, a gift from the people of China to the City of Manchester, was built, erected, and decorated by a team of craftsmen and engineers from Beijing. In recognition of the magnificence of this gift, it was officially opened by his Royal Highness Prince Philip, Duke of Edinburgh, Consort to the Queen of England.'

With open-mouthed, drop-jawed surprise, and shrieks of disbelief, they pressed closer, almost suffocating him. An elbow struck him above his right temple as a mobile phone was thrust high to capture the moment. He found it impossible to move.

'Note the exquisite decorations of the arch which include areas of Chinese ceramic, lacquer, paint, and layers of gold leaf. This arch symbolises the hopes of the People of China for the peace, prosperity, and health of the city.' The umbrella whirled several times above her head before stabbing to the right. 'The final perfect accompaniments are the ornamental gardens behind me, and the two pavilions in which we are invited to rest. But we do not have time to rest. First, we must eat.' Umbrella aloft, she turned on her heel, and marched away.

With an excited cheer, the crowd surged after her like a swarm of chattering locusts. For a moment he feared they might carry him with them. Instead they swirled past, leaving him standing dazed and alone.

Uncertain of his bearings, he turned right beneath the arch and headed on up Faulkner Street past the New Hong Kong Restaurant. Hunger caused his belly to rumble; fear caused the pulse in his neck to begin to throb."

The Tiger's Cave

On your left is Ho's Bakery. Well worth a visit, whether or not you intend to have a coffee and sample some of their glorious sweet and savoury cakes, buns, and pastries. In fairness, and in case you're not quite ready for a break, I should point out that Wong Wong bakery on Princess Street, just a few doors up from the Yang Sing, is equally superb. You'll be passing it on your return journey to the car park.

Continue left past Ho's Bakery entrance, until you reach the junction with George Street. **[K]**. Beside you, Pearl City International Buffet offers probably the most comprehensive such buffet in Britain, if not Europe. Caton brought SOCA Agent Ray Barnes here to try to sate his impressive appetite.

Ray Barnes speared a pan fried pork and prawn dumpling, swirling it slowly in the dipping sauce.

Caton lifted his spoon of Beijing hot and sour soup, blew ripples across the surface, and savoured the clash of flavours; yin and yang.

'I wouldn't be too hard on yourself,' the Agent crunched through the crispy shell, into the soft and succulent flesh beneath. 'There was quite a bit of dissembling going on in there if you ask me. It stood out a mile that he was Fujianese, or at the very least not from Hong Kong. It was just a way of keeping you on the back foot.'

'Well at least we have a name, and symbol to go at.' Caton held his spoon suspended above the bowl. 'And why do I have a feeling you've been saving something up to tell me?'

Ray Barnes grinned. 'Three of the bodies at the sandpits also had tattoos. None of them identical, but the same kind of thing; family or given name in representative form.'...

...The Agent turned his attention to a shredded duck roll in bean curd leaves. 'It looks that way. And another thing; from the clothes, and a few personal possessions the perpetrators overlooked, we have no doubt those five were newly in from Fujian Province.'

Caton let the final mouthful slide slowly down his throat, put down the spoon, picked up his chopsticks, and stabbed the air with them to make his point. 'Too much of a coincidence. And didn't you say you were surprised that there were only five bodies. Too few to make a shipment worthwhile?'

'Exactly so...I tell you what though, this food is seriously good.'

They ate in silence for a minute. Enjoying the food; considering the options.

...A waiter appeared with the final two dishes. He placed them on the table with due ceremony.

'Steamed pieces of chicken, with fish maw; Chinese mushrooms and crab stick; steamed tripe, marinated with oyster sauce. Please enjoy.'

Caton stared at the small attractive dishes with a rising sense of guilt. His team were slaving away, and here he was indulging. He consoled himself with the thought that it would be late evening before he ate again, and raised the chopsticks. Barnes got there first. The tripe squirmed between the ivory sticks, slipped back into the sauce, and peppered the tablecloth with spots of reddish brown. It reminded Caton that there were probably others still out there, hunted by the men that had put Feng in the mortuary. He wiped his mouth with his napkin, and finished the mineral water in his glass. His appetite had deserted him. "

The Tiger's Cave

Cross Nicholas Street, and head up George Street with the car park on your right-hand side. After 50 yards, on your right, is the Woo Sang Supermarket [L]. Pop in if you happen to be looking for a wok, chop sticks, or some oriental sauces, and much much more. Immediately beyond it, on the corner, is Caton's favourite Chinese eatery, the Little Yang Sing, an offshoot of its famous older sibling. [M].

Turn left here, and head up Charlotte Street for 70 metres. On the opposite side of the street, by the traffic lights for Mosley Street, is the door to the Portico Library. **[N].** You can't miss it; there is a blue plaque on the wall beside it, and the name and date – 1806 – on the stone lintel above the doorway. Cross the street, press the speaker button, announce your wish to visit, and push the door, which will open to give you access to the narrow stairway up to the library. Unfortunately the physical constraints of this historic building prevent access for wheelchair users.

The Portico is open from 9.30 – 16.30 Monday Tuesday, Wednesday, and Friday, 9.30 – 19.30 on Thursday, and 11.00 to 15.00 on Saturdays. It is open to the public, and admission is free. Tea or coffee and cake are available from the kitchen all day, and freshly homemade soup and sandwiches are available from 12.00 to 14.00. You can enjoy them at the tables in the Gallery under the dome, surrounded by bookshelves, or in the tiny Victorian Reading Room in the rear. It's worth a visit to see the elegant glass dome, the inspirational exhibition space in the Gallery, and even the original Victorian toilet on the stairs.

Opened in 1806 as a subscription Newsroom and Library, the Portico met the needs of local business men and worthies during the boom years of Georgian and Victorian Manchester, whose literary works it now houses in abundance. Famous members, and former members, of the library include Sir Robert Peel, John Dalton, Roget of Roget's Thesaurus, Elizabeth Gaskell's husband, Tony Booth, Val McDermid, Guy Garvey [lead singer of Elbow], Mike Harding, and Stuart Maconie. Although not in the same league, you may just come across me researching for my next DCI Caton Manchester Murder Mystery.

Leave the Portico, cross back over Charlotte Street, and walk 135 yards down Mosley Street, to arrive at the entrance to the Manchester City Art Gallery. **[O]**. The Gallery is open from 10am to 5pm every day, including bank holidays, with late night opening on Thursdays to 9pm. Entry is Free. Donations are welcomed.

Accessibility: There are three disabled parking spaces on Nicholas Street, 10 metres from the ramped access to the main entrance on Mosley Street. There are also three spaces on Princess Street, 50 metres from the main entrance ramp. Wheelchair and buggy access is via the ramp on Nicholas Street. The gallery is completely accessible for both wheelchairs and buggies. Motorised and manual wheelchairs are available in the entrance hall. There is also a wheelchair lift at the groups entrance on Princess Street. There are lifts to all floors, and accessible toilets with baby changing facilities on the ground and first floors.

The Manchester Art Gallery is home to the city's world-class art collection, containing 25,000 objects of fine art, decorative art, and costume – in the Costume Gallery. The building itself is an architectural masterpiece in the way in which is combines neoclassical and modern design. It has a strong educational ethos with regular workshops for children of all ages, and hands on interactive exhibits. Tel: 0161 235 8888 or visit the website for details of special exhibitions or interactive activities for children. There is also a cafe serving hot and cold food.

Tom and Kate Caton pop in whenever they are in this part of the city, especially when there is a new exhibition. No surprise then that it appears in the series from time to time.

"The sky was clear. A bitter cold wind had swept in from the Urals, threatening snow on the Pennine heights and sleet down here in the centre of the city. Oblivious, he started walking aimlessly, up past the Bridgewater Hall, straight across Oxford Street, into Portland Street. At the junction with Princess Street he turned left and walked the short distance to the Manchester Art Gallery. For almost an hour he wandered through the galleries, losing himself in familiar paintings, barely aware of his surroundings. He stopped before a painting by Valette that had always seemed to him to

epitomise the historic soul of the city. In the foreground, a cellar man trundled his barrow across a fog-bathed Albert Square. In the middle ground, the Albert Memorial, and the statues of Oliver Heywood – banker, philanthropist and first Freeman of the city – and Victorian Prime Minister William Gladstone, looked down upon the scene. In the middle distance, horse-drawn cabs and motor cars vied with each other and with the perilous tramlines. Soot-blackened, the town hall loomed above them all. "

A Fatal Intervention

Leave the Art Gallery, and turn left down Princess Street. Walk ahead for 200 yards, passing Ho's bakery and the Yang Sing across the road on your right just before you cross Portland Street. Carry on down Princess Street for another 90 yards, then turn left into Major Street. After 125 yards you will arrive back at Chorlton Street car park.

If you arrived by train, or bus, or Metrolink, turn left out of the Manchester Art Gallery, cross Princess Street, and continue for 120 yards into St Peter's Square where you will find Metrolink, and Metro Shuttle buses to take you back your mainline stations.

Walk 4
Castlefield Urban Heritage Park.

Associated Titles:
The Cleansing, The Frozen Contract, The Tiger's Cave, A Venetian Moon.

This is a circular walk around the world's first Urban Heritage Park. A status earned on account of the close proximity of the remains of a Roman fort and settlement, the world's first modern industrial canal, the world's first passenger railway terminus, and the Museum of Science and Industry [MOSI] - a complex of museums dedicated to Manchester as the first city of the Industrial Revolution, and the region's Industrial and scientific past, and future.

The first area of the city's Roman and industrial heritage to be regenerated, of unique historical and scientific interest, and visually striking, Castlefield is also blessed with eleven bars, restaurants, and gastro pubs. There is something here for everyone. No wonder that Tom Caton chose to buy his first bachelor pad right here.

The Walk
Ideal as a short walk, or a half day or a full day when combined with visits to the MOSI complex incorporating: The Museum of Science and Industry; The Air and Space Museum; Liverpool Road Station; and The City Underground.

Distance: 1.3 miles
Time: 45 minutes

Allow an additional half a day for exploration of MOSI, especially if accompanied by children or young people. Also allow time for lunch or dinner in one of the many fine restaurants and bars.

Terrain: Pavements and pedestrianised streets, steps, bridges, and cobbles. Easy Walking. See also **Access issues** below.

Getting There:
By car: Head for City Centre and then follow the signs for Castlefield.

Car parking: The Museum of Science and Industry car park - M3 4FP - is open from 8.30 am until 6 pm Monday - Friday and from 9.50 am – 6 pm on Saturday and Sunday. Car parking on-site costs £4.50 for the day. A limited number of Blue Badge slots are available. Get there early! The next nearest are: Water Street, Manchester M3 4JU, and Stone Street NCP at M3 4NE . These are also the cheapest, and very popular. There is always room at The Great Northern Warehouse M3 4EE, but at twice the cost. For those planning to eat at The Wharf Bar and Restaurant there is free parking accessed from Blantyre Street. Similarly for Albert's Shed, and Dukes 92, off Castle Street, and the Choice Bar, off Chester Road.

By Train: Deansgate Station is the nearest, just a five minute walk to the start. Salford Station is a just under half a mile away. About a 12 minute walk away. The FREE Metro Shuttle Route 2* runs from Victoria Station to the start on Liverpool Road.

By tram: Deansgate-Castlefield -formerly GMEX – is the nearest Metrolink station. Serviced by trams travelling to and from Altrincham, MediaCity UK, St Werburgh's Road, and Eccles, but not from Bury. It is a just over 400 metres walk from the station to the start of this walk.

By Bus: Alight at the junction of Deansgate and Liverpool Road, opposite the Beetham Tower/Hilton hotel. The FREE Metro Shuttle Route 2* stops her from Victoria Station.

*Note. There is no Metro Shuttle service on a Sunday or Public Holiday.

Access issues:

Access to much of the site for wheelchair users, and others with limited mobility is possible, although restricted in places by the stepped bridges. To avoid these, the best access points are Bridgewater Street – off Deansgate – giving access to the Roman Remains and the Castlefield Arena; Castle Street, also off Deansgate, giving access to the main canal basin, Albert's Shed, Dukes 92, the Castlefield Arena, and Roman Remains; and Blantyre Street, off the A57 Dawson Street, giving access to Slate Wharf.

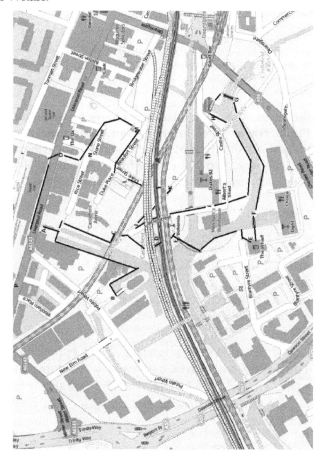

© OpenStreetMap contributors - opendatacommons.org

Start On Liverpool Road, at the head of the steps leading down to the Castlefield Canal Basin **(A).** On your right is the **Castlefield Hotel and Y Club**. Behind you is part of Museum of Science and Industry Building.

From this vantage point you can see the tuning fork prongs of the Staffordshire Warehouse Wharf. The Staffordshire Wharehouse has been replaced by the events arena, complete with the wavelike canopy. It was in this arena that Caton and thousands of other Mancunians, received the news of the City's failed Olympic bid, and with characteristic Mancunian spirit burst into the Monty Python song: "Always Look On The Bright Side of Life." The reward for this optimism was to be the staging of the Commonwealth Games, a far less costly, and much friendlier Games.

"A discordant clash of tubular bells caught his attention as he passed Potato Wharf. Three brightly painted narrowboats nestled close in the basin. Beside them, a gang of men at the foot of the stepped arena were unloading scaffolding poles from a wagon. Whatever the event, he hoped it wasn't going to be as loud as the last one."

The Cleansing.

Proceed down the three flights of steps. On your right is the entrance to the Y Club [YMCA}Sports and Social Club where Tom Caton is a long term member, and I trained during my 18 years working in the city. On the wall, on your left, are two plaques. The first reads:

"Staffordshire Warehouse Bridgewater Canal opened in 1764. Note: [The first 7 miles to Castlefield were completed in 1761] *Immediately, new industrial buildings sprang up all over the area. The face of Castlefield had changed. The Industrial Revolution had arrived."*

At this point, turn right and head alongside the Y Club, for 100 metres, passing under the redbrick Railway bridge. Follow the towpath alongside the YMCA hostel, and Potato Wharf, and after 30 metres turn left to arrive at a bridge leading to a building on an island. **(B).**

Beneath this bridge you will see a large circular weir. Formerly known as Cloverleaf Weir on account of its shape, it's purpose was, and still is, to remove excess water from the canal and drain it into the Medlock River which runs in a tunnel underneath Castlefield, and the city. The last time I was here a fisherman on this bridge was landing small Roach at a rate of two fish a minute. Further evidence of the improved water quality throughout the Castlefield, Medlock, Irwell, and Manchester Ship Canal network.

Retrace your route to the foot of the steps where you began. Now walk straight ahead along the towpath beside the arena, heading for the black and white steel bridge just visible beside the railway arches. **(C).** Turn left up the steps. Before you cross the bridge, look to your left at the narrow canal arm beneath the bridges. **(D).** This is popularly known as **Cropper's Corner**, as it was here that Coronation Street villain Tony Gordon attempted to drown Roy Cropper. Now cross the bridge. Walk straight ahead for 10 metres. To your left is the Barca Bar whose balcony and outside tables are packed with revellers throughout the summer months. Arrive at the impressive Merchant's Footbridge. **(E).**

As you cross the bridge notice on your right the complex of viaducts carrying George Stephenson's original railway, and two subsequent lines. At this point you also have two canals meeting, and a river flowing beneath. Proof, if needed, that this was the first true Industrial transport hub in the world. To your left note the soaring glass and steel structure that is the Beetham Tower. Housing the Hilton Hotel and its famous Cloud bar, it was also home to the Ying Zheng Xiong, the mercurial Chief Executive of the Manchester and Shanghai Trading Corporation in The Tiger's Cave.

Turn left at the end of the bridge, down the steps, and turn left to read the plaque on the wall. For the benefit of wheelchair users the text is repeated below:

"By 1776 the Bridgewater Canal had been extended 28 miles West to meet the Mersey Estuary at Runcorn, giving Castlefield a direct link to the sea. During the 19th Century the North Wales quarries shipped vast quantities of slate to Manchester to roof hundreds of new factories and thousands of new homes. This area was Slate Quay. Demand for building materials was immense. Between 1801 and 1901 the population of Manchester grew from 70,000 to 544,000."

Note: During this period Manchester was the fastest growing city in the world.

To your left at this point, on the opposite side of the canal basin, is the Merchant's Warehouse. Built in the 1820's it is one of the earliest remaining warehouses. The two large arches mark the former under-cover loading bays.

Continue along the canal towpath, or down the gentle paved slope, to arrive at The Wharf bar and restaurant. **(F).** You are now on **Jackson's Wharf**. Do take the time to enter The Wharf bar, and prepare to be surprised. In common with other bars and restaurants in Castlefields it is a sympathetic refurbishment which celebrates the historical importance of this area. There are framed prints on the walls, and cosy rooms with open fires, leather seats, and well stocked book shelves. It also serves a superb range of real ales, and great pub grub in a warm and friendly atmosphere. In the summer especially, expect to find this and all the other bars crammed to the rafters.

"Caton jerked awake. The pain was excruciating. His right calf was knotted with cramp. He swung his feet to the floor and massaged his leg roughly, angling his toes towards the ceiling until the tension eased and the pain subsided. The television flickered blankly. It was dark outside. He looked at his watch. Already ten to seven. He switched off the TV and went to pull the blinds. Down

on the quays, noisy revellers would already be making their way to Dukes 92, Barca, Albert's Shed and Jackson's Wharf."

The Cleansing.

Leave the Wharf and immediately cross the wooden bridge ahead of you. **(G).** On your right is the Middle Warehouse and Basin. The warehouse, which also had covered loading and unloading docks, is home to Key 103 radio station, and The Choice Bar, an award winning modern British restaurant. On Manchester United match days it is possible to combine a 2 course meal here with a return canal cruise to Old Trafford.

Now continue straight ahead along the tow path with the Castle Basin on your left-hand side. Cross the flat wood and iron bridge ahead of you **(H),** turn left, and walk up the steps and onto the Grocer's Warehouse Bridge, constructed in 1990 during the refurbishment of Castlefield. Head 10 yards to the left arriving at the twin flat black and white bascule bridges spanning a short arm of the canal. Bascules are basically drawbridges that use a counterweight to balance the span of the bridge as it swings upwards to allow the barges to pass beneath.

The building ahead of you with the tall tower is the Grocer's Warehouse. Inside the two arches of this warehouse cargo was raised from the barges directly into the warehouse using a winch that was powered by the River Medlock it its tunnel beneath the canal. Regular demonstrations are held of the replica waterwheel and winding gear. The river can still be heard flowing through the chamber, both here, and through the air vents that sit immediately above you and behind the warehouse, on the Castle Street.

Walk down the steps **(I),** and walk along the tow path with the canal basin now on your left. Where the tow path turns to the right away from the canal follow it for 40 metres and climb the steps ahead and to the left of you. At the top of the steps, on your left, you will see the rear of the Merchant's Warehouse. Immediately ahead of you is **Albert's Shed** restaurant. Continue ahead with Albert's Shed on your right, and the Merchant's Warehouse on your left. Pause when you reach the front of Albert's Shed, with Duke's 92, to the right of you.

Dukes 92 is named after the Lock 92, whose Lock Keeper's House is on your left on the other side of the canal. Dukes 92 was the first restaurant and bar to be opened in Castlefield. Both Duke's and Albert's Shed are immensely and justifiably popular. Dukes for its relaxed bar and grill atmosphere and food, and Albert's Shed for the first class British Cuisine, with an Italian twist. There is as a true story attached to its name. In the early 1990s the building was an all but derelict stable used by Albert, the uncle of the owner, to store tools and materials used in the conversion of Duke's 92. He agreed to vacate the shed on condition that the restaurant that was to replace it be named after him. How cool is that?

"They had a table in the window of Albert's Shed, looking out at the former lock keeper's house on the opposite bank of the canal. It was a farewell meal for their Italian colleagues.... They left the hustle and bustle of Albert's Shed behind and strolled along the towpath towards the Beetham Tower..."

A Venetian Moon.

Continue straight ahead over the bridge, with the Lock Keeper's House on your right-hand side. The lock is the first on what now becomes the Rochdale Canal as the canal heads off under Deansgate, and across the city towards the Pennine Hills.

"There was a full moon almost identical to the one they had shared on that fateful night at the San Clemente Palace. This time it was a lighter blue, in a sky where the stars were hidden by the glow of the city. Bonifati followed Caton's gaze to the canalside apartments, lit like jewels against the silhouettes of the darkened office blocks...

They walked on for a while, watching the moonlight shimmer on the canal and the reflected street lights dance where the breeze ruffled the surface...An empty lager can lay by his foot on the towpath. He nudged it with the toe of his shoe into the canal.

They watched it float, waiting for the water to discover the hole where the ring pull had been. Slowly it began to fill. Just when it seemed that it might settle there, in suspended animation, it slid silently beneath the surface and descended into the inky depths. A cloud passed across the moon, deepening the darkness as though a light had been extinguished."

A Venetian Moon

Follow the blue signpost directions for **The Roman Fort**, heading under the railway bridges. At the junction, **(K),** turn right, and after 47 yards turn left **(L),** under the arches, and up to the first set of steps that lead to the Roman Remains. **(M).** Walk ahead to read the plaque on the wall entitled "Mancumium, A Slice Of History." This plaque traces the history of the 4 forts that stood on this spot during the 330 years that Roman soldiers occupied this site. Climb the steps on your left up to the top level of the fort and follow the path along to the right. Turn right onto Beaufort Street with new flats on your left-hand side and railway bridges on your right. After 50 yards you will reach the second half of the Roman Remains **(N).** The map on the display board provides a picture of the full extent of the fort and the vicus, or settlement, that surrounded it.

Turn left following the signs for the **Museum of Science and Industry [MOSI]**. Walk straight ahead for 60 yards towards the tall maroon structure. You have now reached Liverpool Road. **(P).**

The small church-like building beside you is St Matthew's Victorian Sunday School, a poignant reminder of the elegant St Matthew's Church designed by Sir Charles Barry who also designed the Palace of Westminster in London and, here in Manchester, the Mosley Street Art Gallery, now the City Gallery, and the Athenaeum club. The church, which stood approximately where MOSI stands now, was demolished in 1951. On your right is the **Ox pub**. Formerly the Oxnoble.

This gastro pub featured in The Cleansing, and subsequent DCI Caton novels.

"The winter sun sent shafts of light spearing in all directions off the steel sphere at the entrance to the Museum of Science and Industry.

Caton turned up the collar of his coat and weaved his way in and out of the river of people streaming into the city centre. He crossed to the other side of Liverpool Road, where the licensee of The Ox, whose gastropub menu and guest beers ensured that Caton was a regular, was busy fixing the watering system for the hanging baskets. Caton wondered how many people in the Whitbread Empire knew that the inn, formerly The Oxnoble, was named after a potato, not an ox. Come to that, would they be pleased to learn that a building at the rear had opened in the 1870s as the Manchester and Salford venereal diseases centre? Would that have threatened or boosted trade, he mused? Out of the clinic and into the pub. Just what they'd need. A good stiffener."

The Cleansing

The iron, steel and glass building opposite the Ox is the **Air and Space Museum**, formerly part of Campsfield Victorian markets. Ahead of you is the Museum of Science and Industry, incorporating the Power Hall, The 1830 Warehouse – the oldest surviving railway building in the world – the Air and Space Museum, and the Liverpool Road Station. As with all the museums in Manchester entry is free, and this is one attraction not to be missed. A celebration of the Industrial Revolution, and Manchester's part in that and in Scientific discoveries to the present day, it includes interactive galleries, working models of machinery, and engines, including Stephenson's Locomotion, on which it is possible to take a short ride down to the Liverpool Road Station.

"Kate stood watching Harry as he raced against the clock to build a tower taller than himself. It had been a stroke of genius to bring him to the Museum of Science and Industry. There was more than enough in the twelve galleries to keep a boy like him occupied for several days, or a girl come to that. And all of it free. Well not quite all of it.

The 4D sensory theatre with its moving seats, blasts of air and water sprays had been worth every penny. The hardest part for Harry had been choosing between blasting off into space and walking on the moon, or Maid Marian's whirlwind journey attempting to escape the clutches of the evil Sheriff of Nottingham. In the end Robin Hood had won. Kate had to admit, she'd secretly enjoyed it immensely herself. Well, not so secretly. Her shrieks and screams had probably given that away, and it was a toss-up as to who had squeezed the other's hand the hardest."

The Frozen Contract

If you walk 240 yards down Liverpool Road you will arrive back at the start. **(A)**

(If you proceed for another 80 yards you will reach, on your right, the Grade 1 listed Liverpool Road Station Building Museum. This was one of two stations – the other in Liverpool - that marked the start and end of the world's very first twin track, timetabled and ticketed, inter city passenger railway.)

Walk 5
Salford Quays and The Lowry

Associated Titles: The Head Case

This is a delightful circular walk around historic Salford Quays, just a 10 minute drive from the City Centre, and easily accessed from the motorway network.

Officially known as the Port of Manchester during its heyday, and unofficially as Manchester Docks, it is now home to Media City, The Lowry Theatre and Lowry Gallery, the Imperial War Museum North, Manchester United Football Club, a Sport England funded Watersports centre, a retail mall, restaurants and bars, hotels, and thousands of waterfront residences in the form of modern houses and apartments.

Link: http://www.thequays.org.uk/

The Walk
Ideal as a short walk, or a half day or a full day when combined with visits to The Imperial War Museum North, the BBC Tour, the Manchester United Tour, or a show at the Lowry Theatre.

Distance:	1.75 miles
Time:	A 50 minute stroll.

Allow an additional half a day for exploration of The Imperial War Museum North, The Manchester United Tour, or the BBC Tour in Media City, which also offers a CBBC Interactive experience for children. For the BBC, and Manchester United, Booking in advance is essential.

Link: http://www.bbc.co.uk/showsandtours/tours/salford_cbbc.shtml

Link: http://www.oldtraffordtour.com/stadium-museum-tour

Terrain: Flat pavements and pedestrianised streets, steps, ramps, and bridges. Easy Walking. See also **Access issues** below.

Getting There:
By car: From the M60 motorway that circles Manchester City Centre, take junction 12 for the M602. Leave the M602 at junction 3, and follow the brown Lowry logo signs, or the signs for media City. Then follow the signs for the Lowry Outlet Mall car park.

Car parking: Park at the Lowry Outlet Mall car park: Pier 8, Salford Quays, M50 3AH.

Tip 1. If you spend £5 or more at any of the permanent retail outlets, including cafes and restaurants, and cinemas, in the mall, ask them to validate your car park ticket for 4 hours free parking.

Tip 2. If you sign up for a free Lowry Outlet discount card at the information desk – it is not a credit card – you will get 10% discount at many of the outlets in a mall, and 20% discount at several of the restaurants.

By Train
Both Piccadilly and Victoria train stations have Metrolink stops, with a direct connection to Salford Quays. Trains arriving at Salford Crescent station connect with the Salford Quays Link bus to Salford Quays. Alight at the Media City UK stop.

For more information visit Link: www.tfgm.com

By Metrolink:
MediaCity UK and Broadway are the two stops closest to the starting point in the Lowry Plaza. Services are frequent and best

picked up at Piccadilly, Victoria, or Salford Crescent railway stations, or at Cornbrook.

For more information visit Link: www.tfgm.com

By Bus. The number 9 Quays Link bus runs from Salford Crescent to The Lowry. Other buses include the 79 from Swinton and Stretford, the 270 and X50 from the Trafford Centre, and the X25 from Preston. Always check with Transport for Greater Manchester for current timetables and routes:
Link: http://www.tfgm.com/Corporate/Documents/ Information/12-0481-Getting-to-Salford-Quays.pdf

Access issues: On the longer walk there are several places where steps or bollards limit   accessibility. A shorter walk, providing views across the majority of the quays and suitable for wheelchair users, is highlighted in italics in the details of the walk below.

"Within weeks of its opening in 1894 Manchester Ship Canal had broken the strangle hold of the exorbitant docks and harbour fees at the port of Liverpool, and made possible the development of Trafford Park – the first and largest industrial estate in the world, from which textile manufacturing machinery was sold across the globe. Ironically, it was the success of those very exports that was to bring about the decline of the Ship Canal itself, and the Manchester docks that it served. Cheap imports of cotton goods made on the machines that had originated here all but destroyed the Lancashire cotton trade.

By the late 1970s these docks were derelict. Over the past two decades Caton had watched them rise like a phoenix from the ashes. Now Salford Quays was a vibrant centre of regional and national significance for its business, enterprise, culture, and sport. The canal basins, and the waterway itself - only a decade before a stagnant mire - now held perch, roach, and pike, so DS Carter assured him. The canal itself - one of the most successful venues of the Commonwealth Games – was the home of the annual World Triathlon Cup. And, miracle of miracles, the BBC was moving five of its major departments from London to Salford's Media City in the centre of this complex. According to Greater Manchester Radio, over one and a half thousand people currently lived here. As of this morning, he reflected grimly, there was one fewer."

The Head Case

Start In the centre of the Lowry Plaza **[A]**, stand facing the Lowry Theatre, with your back to the Lowry Outlet Shopping Mall. Turn right, and head around the tall building with black glazed tiles and black and green windows. Cross at the crossing point on the corner to the side of the Huron Basin. Turn right, and continue ahead with the water on your left-hand side.   On reaching the red Detroit Bridge, **[B]** turn left and cross the bridge.

(**Wheelchair users** *should at this point ignore the bridge and continue ahead, following the Blue Route to the Mariner's Quay [**F**]. They should turn left here continuing along the canal with the water on their left. On reaching the end of the canal [**M**], they should turn right and follow the instructions from this point back to the start.*)

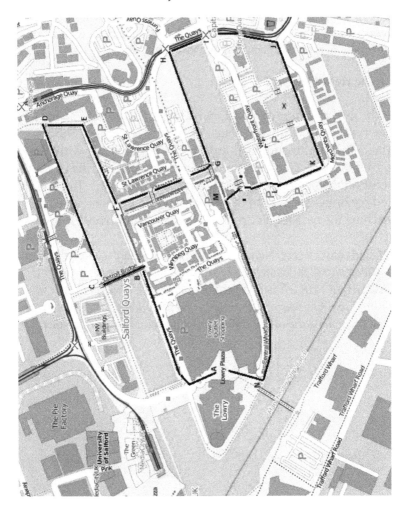

Having crossed the bridge **[C]**, turn right and walk along the side of the Eire Basin with the water on your right. Continue to the end of the Basin **[D]**. Turn right and walk to the opposite side of the Erie Basin **[E]**. Now turn right, and continue along the waterside until you reach the Mariner's Canal **[F]**. Turn left, and walk beside the canal with the water on your right. This stretch has the feel of Amsterdam, with the trees , the cyclists and the joggers. Only the barges are missing. Continue to the end of the canal, [G] and turn left.

Continue along the side of the Ontario Basin with the water on your right. At the end of the Basin [H] turn right and walk along beside the Metrolink tracks. The cream Art Deco building on your left, completed in 1927, was the former Dock Office. Cross Waterfront Quay [I] with care, and continue to the right of, and below, the tram station.

At the end of the Basin [J], turn right by the large circular blue signs and along Merchant's Quay, staying by the water's edge. Continue ahead in a straight line beside St Francis' Basin. The second Basin that you reach is St Louis Basin. [X]. This is where the second victim in The Head Case was discovered.

"The body was barely visible. It was not just the overcast sky and beating rain. High winds had driven a mass of detritus into this corner of the St Louis Basin. The victim, her matted hair, once blonde now filthy brown, floated face up, among the coke cans, plastic bottles, and sodden food wrappers. It was beyond Caton why they hadn't taken her out of the water...

... Benson pointed to one of the houses behind them. A huddle of women stood just inside the doorway at the end of the garden, behind the line of sorbus trees, and a low white picket fence.
'The guy who found her knocked on that door to get them to ring for help. The owner recognised her. Apparently she lived just round the corner on South Bay.' ...

... Caton stayed there for a moment, committing the scene to memory. It would all be captured by the photographs and the video footage. But nothing would adequately reflect the mood of this place, at this moment. Dark, dank, and depressing. But there was something else. He couldn't quite put his finger on it. Normally he would have a sense of foreboding. That this was the beginning, or continuation, of something evil. Not this time."

The Head Case

Continue ahead, to arrive at the far end of the last of these three basins — St Peter's Basin, **[K]**. Turn right, and continue ahead for 160 yards to the car park **[L]** to the left of the hotel – the Holiday Inn Express. Look to your left across the basin. DCI Caton stood on exactly this spot, as he contemplated the grim discovery that had just been made in the St Louis Basin

"He walked to the end of the promenade and looked out across the stretch of open water, down the main canal to where the sun glinted on the sharp edged stainless steel cladding of Daniel Liebkind's futuristic Imperial War Museum North. A flight of swans swooped in, and landed elegantly just yards from where he stood. Suddenly it struck him that this had been neither the beginning of a new evil, nor the continuation of an old one. In some strange way it felt more like an ending. But of what, he had not the faintest idea."

The Head Case

Following the pedestrian signs for the Lowry, and the Watersports Centre, walk down the ramp to the left of the hotel and cross the bridge ahead of you to reach the Watersports Centre **[M]**.

Wheelchair users rejoin the route at this point.

The Watersports Centre provides an exciting range of activities at which it is possible for the able bodied, and those with disabilities, to try their hand. These include wakeboarding, dinghy sailing, kayaking and canoeing, open water swimming, windsurfing, power boating, scuba diving and snorkelling, even climbing and abseiling. Booking in advance is essential. To book onto any of the courses, simply call Salford Watersports Centre on 0161 877 7252.

On the wall on your right is the name plaque for the Agecroft Rowing Club whose home this now is. You may be surprised to learn that rowing clubs have existed on the Manchester and Salford waterways – especially the River Irwell, since the 1820s.

The Agecroft club was formed through the amalgamation of a number of these clubs in 1861, thus making it one of the oldest open membership rowing clubs in the world. Thanks to the first class facilities, and top class coaching, Agecroft now boasts the most successful senior rowing section in the country outside of London.

Before leaving, look for a large granite plaque set into the wall on the left of the Watersports Centre. This is a commemorative plaque in memory of the more than 30,000 merchant seamen who gave their lives setting out from these docks, and others around the United Kingdom, to support the war effort and break the U Boat blockade.

Turn left, and continue along the waterfront with the water on your left hand side. The toast rack like structure on the opposite bank is the Manchester United Old Trafford Stadium – the supposed Theatre of Dreams – at least as far as DS Holmes is concerned.

Look out for the circular stainless steel discs set into the walkway or your left, between the lamp posts. This is Centenary Way which Princess Anne formerly opened in May 1994 to commemorate the opening of the canal by Queen Victoria one hundred years earlier. The words engraved on the discs, that reflect the maritime history of the docks and their modern re-incarnation, are by the poet Su Andi together with local people.

Continue alongside the water and the trees until you reach the foot of the bridge between Central Wharf and Trafford Wharf. **[K].** Turn right, and you have arrived back at the Plaza where you began the walk. **[A].**

You are now free to cross the bridge and walk over to the Imperial War Museum North [350 yards]; or Manchester United's Ground [1,500 metres], visit the Lowry Theatre and Gallery, explore Media City, or shop till you drop in the Mall. If you do buy anything, don't forget to have your parking ticket validated.

Note of Interest. You have just completed 80% of the route followed by the world famous Salford Triathlon. Except of course that those on the Olympic course will have completed a 1500 metre swim, a 6.7 kilometre ride, and a 10 kilometre run. The World Record at the time of going to press is 1 hour 39 minutes and 50 seconds. Just under twice as long as it has taken you to complete 1.75 miles.

Walk 6
Around the Universities – The Cultural Corridor.

Associated Titles: The Cleansing, A Trace of Blood, Bluebell Hollow, Backwash.

About the walk.
The walk takes you south from the city centre and along Oxford Road, through Manchester's so-called cultural corridor. This district is home to two universities, numerous galleries, high-tech research labs and medical facilities, theatres, cinemas, student cafe bars and restaurants, and much more. A place where science, technology, art and culture meet. The place where the atom was first split, the Geiger counter was developed, the world's first stored-program computer was invented, where more than 25 Nobel Prize winners have worked their magic, most recently of whom Andre Geim and Konstantin Novoselov won the Nobel Prize in Physics in 2010 for "... groundbreaking experiments regarding the two-dimensional material graphene." A development that will change our world beyond imagining. Unsurprisingly Manchester University is ranked as one of the top 25 research facilities in the world.

Manchester University and Manchester Metropolitan University, whose buildings populate this campus, boast more than 75,000 full time students, and this is the largest single site concentration of students in Great Britain. Visitors have free access to the grounds, and many of the most significant buildings. Along the way you will have the opportunity to visit The Holden Gallery of Contemporary Art, The Royal Northern College of Music, The Manchester Museum, the historical Sir John Owens Building and the Waterhouse Quad, The Church of the Holy Name, and The Whitworth Art Gallery.

Tom Caton was an undergraduate, and a part-time graduate MA

student in Crime Law and Society, at Manchester University. It was at the university's Henry Fielding Centre of Psychology and Policing that he first met Kate Webb during the Bojangles case. I worked closely for a number of years with both Manchester Victoria and Manchester Metropolitan Universities on mentoring programmes and research, with special emphasis on increasing the admission of pupils from disadvantaged backgrounds. Between us we have pooled our experience to bring you this walk.

Kate's Tip 1: If you visit on a Wednesday you could join one of the Manchester University **guided visits** that start from the Visitor's Centre at 1.30pm and end at approximately 3.30pm. Reservations are essential. To book a place use the following

Link: http://www.manchester.ac.uk/undergraduate/opendays/other-visits/

Kate's Tip 2: You might wish to explore the walk before you come using an interactive map of the cultural corridor.

Link: http://www.corridormanchester.com/explore-the-corridor

Distance:
Total Distance: 1 mile
Total Walking Time: 35 minutes

Allow at least the same amount of time again for exploration of the buildings along the way. Much longer if you attend a concert, or spend a lot of time in the Whitworth Gallery. Even longer if you stop for breakfast, lunch, or afternoon tea in RNCM cafe, Christie's Bistro, or Kro Bar.

Terrain: Pavements and pedestrianised streets. Easy Walking.

Access issues:
All suitable for wheelchair, and mobility scooter access. Christie's Bistro requires the use of a lift. Details are given in the route directions. Wheelchair users will need to be able to access buses or a taxi to return to the car park/start of the walk.

Getting There.
By Car: The Universities are well signposted from all directions as you reach the outskirts of the city. As shown on the map, there are a number of car parks in the vicinity of the start of this walk. We suggest that you make for **Brancaster Road Car Park, M60 7HB.** The directions below will bring you close to the start point but in view of frequent changes to road priorities I suggest that you use your own sat nav or AA/RAC route planning information for the final stage of your journey.

From the M56 South of Manchester, keep in right hand lanes at Junction 3 (signposted City Centre) and continue from the end of the M56 onto A5103 (Princess Parkway), signposted Manchester city centre. Follow signs for the Universities.

From the M60 North and East of Manchester, exit at Junction 22 and turn right at traffic lights onto A62. Continue until the end and turn left onto A665, then follow signs for the Universities

From the M602, West of Manchester, proceed to the end of the M602, join the A57M (Mancunian Way) and leave it at the first exit.

By Rail
From Piccadilly station take the 147 Oxford Rd Link Bus which stops outside the Manchester Technology Centre. This marks the start of the walk. Alternatively, take a train, to Oxford Road station. Turn right out of the station, and right again, to walk 280 yards down to the start of the walk.

From Victoria station take the metrolink tram to Piccadilly station and follow the directions above.

By Bus

Take the 147 bus from Piccadilly railway station to the stop outside the Manchester Technology Centre on Oxford Road. You can also get numerous buses heading towards South Manchester (Bus Number 41, 42, 43, 85, 111, 250, 256), which all stop at or close to the start of the walk.

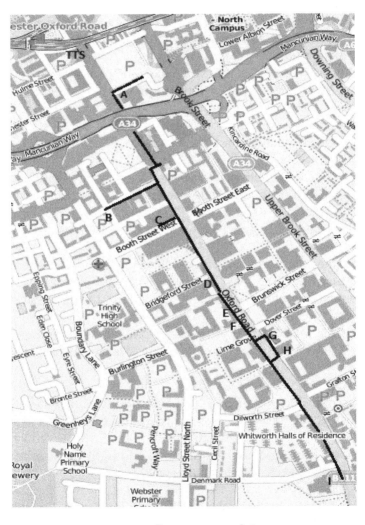

© OpenStreetMap contributors - opendatacommons.org

Start On Oxford Road, at the junction with Brancaster Road. **(A)** Head south down Oxford Road for 300 yards. Stop opposite the furthest end of the green Grosvenor square on your right hand side, at the busy Junction of Grosvenor Street, Oxford Road, and Cavendish Street.

Immediately in front of you, on the corner, is a distinctive building faced with faience and terracotta in green and cream. Opened in 1915 this was the **Grosvenor Picture Palace**. Renamed *Footage*, it still hosts two massive screens, but now together with two Sky Boxes, they bring live sports events to the students who throng the bars. The adjacent Gothic style building on the left of Footage is the former Deaf and Dumb Institute. This has been abbreviated to **The Deaf Institute** and, without a hint of irony, re-incarnated as a Cafe Bar and Music Hall.

Cross at the lights so that you are in front of Footage. Now cross Oxford Road at the lights on your right.

Continue to walk south on Oxford Road for 50 yards, to the end of the building, and then turn right at the blue signposts. Then proceed ahead past The Chatham Building, and the black and glass panelled Benzies Building, both of which belong to the New School of Art until you reach the junction with Higher Ormond Street and Boundary Street. The building on the corner opposite you **[B]** is **The Salutation** pub. A jewel among Manchester's Victorian heritage pubs, with Art Deco features, beloved of lecturers, medics, and locals alike, it was favourite a haunt of Tom Caton in his students days, and was a significant setting in the final chapters of *Backwash*.

"From the outside, the Salutation Hotel and Pub was just as he remembered it. Solidly square, and confident. The ground floor Victorian windows nestled by golden sandstone, those on the upper storey by red brick. Black picnic tables stood behind a wooden fence where the barbecues and music gigs were held. He had heard that the Manchester Metropolitan University had bought it. He hoped they hadn't messed with it.

They hadn't. Rich, red leather Chesterfield seating complemented the original patterned quarry tiled floor. There was the long black ebony bar topped with mahogany, and the beer glass rack suspended on polished brass columns. The old bookcase crammed with books, the wooden plate racks, framed photographs, and the ancient wall clock with the brass surround, and gas style lamps suspended from the ceiling. All still here. But not Adam Davis."

Backwash.

Now owned by Manchester Metropolitan University Student's Union, a complete renovation [Spring 2014], will return it to it's Victorian splendour, including the ornate plaster ceilings and original gas lamps,.

Appropriately refreshed, return to Oxford Road, and turn right to head South once again. Pass two buildings and, on the opposite side of the road the impressive **Manchester Aquatics Centre** built to the host the 2002 Commonwealth Games aquatic events, to reach the busy major junction with Booth Street. Turn right down Booth Street West, to reach the entrance to the **Royal Northern College of Music.[C]**

The RNCM is one of the world's leading international conservatoire, where students are trained to the highest possible level in music through specialised learning programmes delivered by internationally renowned teachers and mentors, and supported by a unique performance programme. Its roots can be traced to the foundation of the Royal Manchester College of Music by Sir Charles Hallé in 1893.

Kate's Tip 3 : The RNCM offers a series of free lunchtime concerts throughout the season. [University Term Time.] This includes solo and duo recitals taking place most Mondays, orchestras and ensembles on Thursdays, and chamber music on selected Fridays. During refurbishment venues may vary so it is essential to check the link below for details. While here why not have lunch or afternoon tea in the Brodsky restaurant, or the RNCM Cafe and Bar. **Link: http://www.rncm.ac.uk/ series/lunchtime-concerts/** You could also visit the Historical Instrument Collection.

Return to Oxford Road, turn right, crossing Booth Street West, and continue south for 200 Yards. Stop at the far end of the row of 7 redbrick terraced houses by the name plate, **'Waterloo Place'**. These Grade 2 Listed houses were built in 1832, and now house offices , including those for the ESRC Centre for Research on Socio-Cultural Change. On the opposite side of Oxford Road the redbrick building is the **Kilburn Building**, named after Tom Kilburn, co- inventor with Frederic Williams, of the world's first stored program computer, and housing the School of Computer Science. Another building in the name of Alan Turing, their collaborator, who helped to shorten the war through his work on the Enigma machine at Bletchley Park, and who is acknowledged as the father of theoretical computer science and artificial intelligence, is at the rear of the Kilburn Building.

 Alan Turing was actively gay at a time when homosexuality was a criminal offence. He was convicted of gross indecency, and chose chemical castration rather than a jail sentence. Within two years he had committed suicide by injecting cyanide into an apple, and taking a bite. He received, belatedly, a Queen's Pardon on 24th December 2013.   in addition to the Alan Turing Building, Alan Turing Way between the Emirates Stadium and the Commonwealth Velodrome, and the famous Apple logo – the apple with the bite taken out – serve as permanent reminders of his genius and immeasurable contributions to Britain and the world.

"They parked at the Commonwealth Games Aquatics Centre, stepped out onto the Oxford Road pavement teeming with students and walked the couple of hundred yards down to the slatted red-brick box that was the Kilburn Building. A sign saying *Access to Computer Science Building* directed them up a winding metal staircase. On the first-floor platform Holmes nudged Caton's arm and pointed diagonally across the road. A banner attached to the

side of the Manchester Museum's Café Muse proclaimed: *Lindow Man. A Bog Body Mystery.*

'Give me one of those any day,' he quipped. 'No witnesses to interview, and the perpetrator's long dead.'

Caton shook his head and started up the second flight.

'Not a lot of call for detectives then,' he said."

Backwash

The large blue steel can of a building, next to the Kilburn Building, is **University Place**. Home to the University Visitor Centre, it also houses the largest dedicated lecture theatre in Greater Manchester, a cafe, and a study zone complete with comfy couches and clusters of computers. Worth a visit in its own right, some of the lectures here are open to members of the public.

Waterloo Place is the start of the historic heart of the University. The building immediately ahead of you is the **Manchester Museum**. **[D]**. You have first to make it past the enticing lead topped portico entrance to the museum's **Café Muse**. Assuming you do make it the fifteen yards to the entrance of the museum, go inside prepared to be surprised. Owned and run by the University behind its turreted façade it houses an enormous collection of artefacts. There 15 galleries covering history – prehistoric to modern - archaeology, geology, natural history, live animals, and much more. If you have children with you they will have a great time. This family friendly museum was joint winner of the Clore Award for Museum Learning 2012.

Link: http://www.museum.manchester.ac.uk/yourvisit/galleries/

Leave the museum and turn right. Walk for 100 yards down Oxford Road to reach the entrance to the quadrangle of the **John Owens Building**. **[E]**.

"It was a dry, crisp morning. Caton waited patiently to turn off Oxford Road and into the car park on Burlington Street, alongside

Alfred Waterhouse's magnificent Whitworth Hall, its walls, buttresses and blue-topped spires gleaming gold and red in the morning sun. He watched as gaggles of students made their way towards the Students' Union Building, just as he had done two decades earlier. He envied their easy camaraderie, their youth and the boundless opportunities ahead of them.

Those had definitely been the best years of his life to date; the friendships, the sport, the MadChester scene, the demos, even the learning. Then, he remembered, we worried about Terry Waite, Northern Ireland, the Lockerbie Bombing, whether the Iran/Iraq war would escalate, Black Monday, Apartheid, the Palestinian–Israeli conflict, Section 28, if Morrissey or New Order would make it to number one. Now, they probably worry about global warming, AIDS in Africa, Iraq, Afghanistan, the Palestinian–Israeli conflict and how to pay off student loans, afford a house and save for pensions. I don't think I'd swap after all, he decided as a break appeared in the traffic. He swung into the narrow street and up to the barrier.

Caton wondered how Kate Webb had managed to wangle him a parking permit, right here in the heart of the Owens complex. He picked the campus map off the dashboard, locked the car and set off on foot to cross Oxford Road and find the Henry Fielding Centre of Psychology and Policing."

The Cleansing

In 1851 John Owens, a wealthy cotton manufacturer founded Owens College in Quay Street Manchester. You pass it early on in Walk 1 in this book. In 1869 Alfred Waterhouse, who also designed Manchester Town Hall – was commissioned to design on this spot a campus of the rapidly expanding college. This part of the building was completed in 1871, and not surprisingly has listed status. Unless you have signed up for one of the Wednesday free tours of the university, simply take your time to wander around the quads soaking up the atmosphere and admiring the buildings.

One way to do this, and at the same time enjoy excellent food and drink in unique surroundings, is to visit the first floor Christie's Bistro in the Old Quadrangle.

Those requiring wheelchair access should start just inside the Quadrangle with their backs to the entrance, and then proceed to their left alongside the buildings to the Christie Building in the left hand corner. Pass through the unmarked wooden door, turn right inside, and pass through the double doors. You will find a modern glass and steel lift immediately ahead of you.

Those without access needs should walk around the Christie Building to reach a stepped entrance on the left. **[F]**. This is normally, but not always, marked by display signs for the Bistro. Climb the steps and follow the signs up the winding stone staircase to reach the Christie Library and Bistro.

Originally part of the Christie Library the lounge has huge brown leather sofas in a room lined with wooden panels and shelves full of books. Connected to the lounge is the modern Christie's Bistro restaurant offering locally and ethically sourced food at competitive prices. Very popular among university staff and those in the know, it is best to book for lunch.

Link: http://www.chancellorshotel.co.uk/chancellors-at-chrisites-menu
[The misspelling of the name in this link is not mine]

Kate's Tip 4:
Before exiting onto Oxford Road check if the **Whitworth Hall** – immediately on the right of the impressive stone arched entrance - is open to visitors. If so, pop in and have a look at this impressive Grade 11 listed building, much used for graduation ceremonies, conferences, banquets, dinner dances, and civil weddings. Request use of the lift if required.

Leaving the Quadrangle, head south again down Oxford Road. After 50 yards cross the first junction, and stop at the *third* crossing point on Oxford Road outside the large steel and glass **Alan Gilbert Learning Commons Building**. This is a state of the art study and learning centre boasting an onsite café, an impressive atrium providing a social meeting space with wifi access and flexible study spaces. Visitors are welcome to use the cafe facilities. Now cross Oxford Road. The white building in front of you is **Kro Bar**. **[G].**

Kro is the re-creation of a Danish village pub. Owned and run by the Ruby family from Jutland, The Kro empire was founded by Borge Ruby who was chef for the King of Denmark on the Royal Yacht. His son Mark was chef at the Royal Hotel in Copenhagen, and on the QE2. The first Kro Bar opened in 1999. There are now four Kro Bars in the city. There is a Breakfast menu until 3pm, and a restaurant menu from 11am. Great food, sensible prices, lots of offers, and a special atmosphere.

Tom's Tip. NB. The best tables are in the first floor rooms, outside at the front under the heated canopies, or, in summer, outside in the beer garden. The Fish Platters and the Meat Platters are especially good value.

Kate's Tip 5: Check the website for offers before you come. If you're a Mancunian sign up for the Kro Club Card. Just £3 with lots of offers in all of the Kro Bars. **Link:** http://www.kro.co.uk/

As you leave Kro Bar take a moment to look across the road at the huge white stone building. This is the **Steve Biko Manchester Student's Union Building**, named after the South African Anti Apartheid activist. (During Caton's time at the university Manchester University Students were at the forefront of the Free Mandela campaign in Britain.) Completed in 1956 I think it has a look of 1930's Art Deco, without the Art. It would not have looked out of place in pre-war Berlin. But among other things it is home to the **Manchester Academy**.

Manchester Academy is a brand name for the four concert venues run by the University of Manchester Students' Union on the Corridor. Manchester Academy 2&3 and Club Academy are inside the Students' Union building. Manchester Academy 1 is in a purpose built redbrick and coloured glass building at the far end of the Biko Building, behind the RBS bank.

For more than half a century Manchester Academy has been an iconic music venue for popular signed bands, and unsigned bands alike, including Ian Brown, The Stranglers, Joe Cocker, The Who, Dire Straits, Pink Floyd, Velvet Underground, The Pretenders, Oasis, Nirvana, Coldplay, The Gorillaz, Dido and Katy Perry. Ian Brown, The Stranglers, Super Furry Animals, Deftones, Pink Floyd, The Cure, The Coral, Blur, Oasis, The Ramones, Billy Talent, Fightstar, Lost Prophets, George Clinton, Nirvana, Manic Street Preachers, Death Cab for Cutie, The Libertines, Babyshambles, Lee "Scratch" Perry, Courtney Love, Supergrass, and It Bites. Just one of the reasons that Manchester is such a popular choice for aspiring undergraduates.

Continue south for 50 yards to reach the **Church of the Holy Name. [H].** The largest church in Manchester, completed in 1871, the Holy Name was founded, and is still run, by the Society of Jesus – the Jesuits. It serves the university community, and is an official Manchester Universities' Chaplaincy. Do have a look inside. Impressive in daylight, at night the lamps and candles highlight the golden chancel and the church has a wonderful ethereal ambience. **Wheelchair Access** is round to the right of the church in Ackers Street.

Kate's Tip 6: The *Carols By Candlelight Concert* must surely rival that of King's College Chapel Cambridge. Not surprising, given the proximity of the Royal Northern College of Music many of whose vocal studies and opera students are regular choir members. If you don't believe me, try this link, and watch the video.

Link: http://www.holyname.info/carols-by-candlelight.html

Leave the church, turn left, and continue south down Oxford Road. After 70 yards, look to your right across the road. The building set back from the road, with nine huge stacks topped with H-shaped chimney pots, is the **Contact Theatre**. Contact Theatre is a voluntary charitable multi-disciplinary arts centre. Contact's vision is a world where young people are empowered by creativity to become leaders in both the arts and their communities. It seeks to achieve that through the provision of inspirational creative programmes covering drama, dance, comedy and art events aimed at a younger audience, and through Creative Traineeships for 16-18 Year olds.

Continue south for another 260 yards to arrive, just past the entrance to the red and white faced facade of the Old St Mary's Hospital, opposite the driveway to the Manchester University **Whitworth Art Gallery**. **[I]**. Cross the road and walk through the green gates, and up the drive to arrive at the impressive Grade 11 redbrick building.

One of the first galleries in England to be built in a park, at the time of writing – April 2104 – the Whitworth is currently undergoing a £15 million redevelopment which will double the public space, expanding existing galleries, and adding a Landscape Gallery, a Promenade and Cafe in the Trees, an Art Garden, and an Orchard Garden. While the gallery is closed feel free to explore the park. If you've brought sandwiches with you, or picked some up along the way, this is a great place to have a picnic.

The Gallery will re-open on Saturday 25th October 2014. Check the link below for current programmes, exhibitions, and events.

Link: http://www.whitworth.manchester.ac.uk/

Leave the Whitworth Gallery. Out on Oxford Road look across the road and to your right. At the end of the row of red brick buildings that are still part of the original St Mary's Hospital, is housed the St Mary's Sexual Assault Referral Centre. One of the foremost and first of such centres in the country, SARC provides comprehensive and co-ordinated forensic, counselling and aftercare to men, women and children who have experienced recent or historic rape or sexual assault. The Centre featured in *A Fatal Intervention*.

"'Robert Thornton, a leading junior counsel, who has appeared on this channel on a number of occasions and has some impressive successes behind him, both for the defence and the prosecution, was arrested this morning at his apartment and taken to Bootle Street Police Station, where he was questioned for several hours. We can now go live to Libby Adamovski at St Mary's Hospital.'

'Thank you, Kerry. Yes, I have just learnt that in the early hours of this morning a young woman, in her twenties, was brought by the police here, to the Sexual Assault Referral Centre, as a victim of serious sexual assault. Three hours later, Robert Thornton, a Manchester barrister, was arrested by the police at his apartment in the centre of the city and taken to Bootle Street Police Station, where he was questioned. I have to emphasise that he was not charged with any offence, but was released at midday, on police bail, pending further enquiries. I have been told that a condition of the bail is that he is to report to Bootle Street Station on a daily basis.'"

A Fatal Intervention

Your walk is now concluded. You have two choices. You can hop on one of the many buses that ply Oxford Road, and be back at the car park or Oxford Road station within a few minutes or, if you're ready for a meal, you can continue a quarter of a mile south along Oxford Road to the start of the famous **Curry Mile** in Rusholme where more than 70 restaurants, sweet shops, and takeaways await your custom. Choose from Indian, Pakistani, Sri Lankan, Bangladeshi and Middle East cuisine.

Postscript.

And finally, If you happen to be returning to Oxford Road Railway Station, have a look under the arches on your left **[TTS]** where you'll find **The Thirsty Scholar**. One of Manchester's best free music venues. They serve food and drink too!

"'Then we decided to go out for a drink,' said Becky. 'Imran said he'd come too.'

She saw the lift of his eyebrows.

'Not alcohol. He came for the company. And the non-alcoholic cocktails.' She smiled thinly. 'To be honest, I quite like some of those myself.'

'Where did you go?'

'To Alibi, on Oxford Road, near the Circus. They have a good sports bar, and loads of screens. There was a Champions League match on. We were there till ten thirty, then we went down to the Thirsty Scholar.'

It was good choice, Caton reflected. Tucked under the viaduct arches by Oxford Station, it had been a favourite haunt for almost two decades, and was still one of the best free live band venues in the city, with great beers and decent food."

Backwash

Further Afield

Two longer walks based on DCI Caton crime scenes, one several miles to the East of the city, the other 11 miles to the West.

Walk 7
Debdale Park and The Monastery and Friary of St Francis, Gorton.

Associated Titles: Backwash, The Tiger's Cave

A Sunday outing that combines a short walk of 2.5 miles around picturesque Debdale Park and Gorton Reservoirs, and a visit to the unique former Franciscan Friary of St Francis Gorton. The walk around Debdale Park and the Reservoirs is described first, followed by an introduction to St Francis, Gorton. Decide for yourself which order to do them in, but ensure that you leave enough time for your visit to the Monastery. [Open most Sundays from 12.00 until 4.00pm.]

Getting There
By Car:
Because there are two sites both with car parks, one and a half miles apart, they are best reached by car. For the walk, park at, or close to, Debdale Outdoor Centre. 1073 Hyde Road, Gorton, Manchester, Opposite McDonalds, just off the A57: M18 7WY Phone: 0161 223 5182.

By Bus
Both sites are on multiple bus routes. Check with the Transport for Greater Manchester Route Finder website:
http://www.tfgm.com/journey_planning/Pages/local_bus_stop_finder.aspx

By Train
There is an hourly train service from Manchester Piccadilly to Fairfield station. [No Sunday service]. The Manchester to Glossop Line trains stop at Gorton, but bypass Fairfield station. If arriving by train begin the walk from Fairfield Station, picking it up at point **E** on the route shown on the map.

The Walk.

Debdale Park is located in Gorton just three miles from the city centre, Debdale Park is a green haven in an otherwise busy urban area and a popular location for water sports. Set in 130 acres, Debdale offers extensive sports and leisure facilities including tennis courts, bowling greens, a basketball court, football pitches and 5-a-side grass pitch, a skateboarding ramp and a children's play area. The nearby reservoirs provide opportunities for fishing and boating, with a dedicated water sports and outdoor activity centre too. Its location adjacent to Gorton reservoirs means that it is a natural home to a great diversity of wildlife. Wooded areas are managed to provide a natural habitat for birds and insects with lots of tree cover and numerous bird and bat boxes positioned around the site for children.

Terrain: Flat paths, lanes, metalled roads, and cycle paths. Easy walking.

Access Issues. This walk is suitable for pedestrians and cyclists. The circular route is not possible for wheelchair users due to the metal barriers on the cycle path to deter motorbike users. However the paths within the park are metalled and this would provide and alternative route of up to 1.3 miles

© OpenStreetMap contributors - opendatacommons.org

Start At Debdale Outdoor centre. **[A]** Facing the red Debdale Outdoor Centre sign and green Fire Assembly signs, take the path on your left, past a small concrete bollard, to reach a tunnel. [B]. Pass through the tunnel and follow the path round to the right to join the cycle track that follows the old Fairfield railway line. This is the route thought to have been taken by the perpetrator/s in Backwash. Continue to head north east along this track. After 200 yards another path heads off to the left towards the estate of back to back terraced houses **[X]** that was the setting for the first crime scene in Backwash.

"A police van was broadside across the street. Beyond it Caton could see a BMW paramedic saloon parked at the kerb. There was a handful of women and some kids huddled in the doorways of the terraces.

He switched off the siren and lights, mounted the pavement, eased past the van, and pulled up behind the ambulance. A uniformed officer stood on the step of a neat red-brick two-up-two-down. Caton locked the car and went, warrant card in hand, to meet him."

Backwash

Unless so minded do not take this path, but continue ahead. After 520 yards you will reach the entrance road to Wright Robinson Sports College **[C]**. Cross this and continue ahead as the path meanders across grassland and between the trees on either side.

"Caton put himself in the place of the perpetrator. If he were to turn right out of the victim's property, the alley would take him onto busy Abbey Hey Lane where there were cameras, and lots of people. Turn left, however, and it brought you out at a fifty-metre strip of grassland that led down to a ramshackle industrial estate, and the banks of Gorton Lower Reservoir. From there it was possible to continue left under the cover of trees behind Wright Robinson Specialist College, all the way along the bank of Gorton Upper Reservoir, to cross the narrow strip between the reservoirs beyond where there was plenty of woodland cover. At this point there was a choice between Denton golf course, or the former Fallowfield railway line all the way to Staylbridge, four miles away. In the opposite direction it would lead them undetected, other than by the occasional dog walker or fitness fanatic, all the way to Sale Water Park, or Old Trafford, depending on which branch they decided to take. Six miles or more in either case, with innumerable opportunities to leave the path and disappear into surrounding streets and industrial premises. The rest of the team were making the same computations."

Backwash

After a quarter of a mile, **[D]**, the path bends left, and then right around a new housing estate, before emerging on Booth Road.

Continue through the estate following the blue C85 cycle route signs. On reaching the Fairfield Golf and Sailing Club on your right, **[E]**, turn up the driveway towards the clubhouse. In the car park pass through the narrow opening in the fence beside the Professional's reserved parking space, down the slope, and onto the broad sandy track ahead as it curves right and then left for 200 yards to reach, at a long green metal gate, King's Road/Debdale Lane. **[F]**. Something of a misnomer, this is a broad un-surfaced sandy lane.

Turn right and continue along King's Road/Debdale Lane for three quarters of a mile as it winds along between the two sides of the golf course. The lane bends to the right and crosses the reservoir at this point, although the view is obscured by trees and hedges on either side. 80 yards on the other side of the reservoir you will reach a path on your right which is partly blocked by a long and low black metal barrier. **[G]**. This is the entrance to Debdale Park. Turn right onto this path, and continue for 250 yards. Ignore the sharp right turn and instead follow the path as it curves left along the side of the reservoir. Continue, eventually passing the children's playground on your left. At the junction of paths **[I],** follow, to the right, the path signposted for the Debdale Outdoor Centre. After 270 yards arrive back at the Start.

The Visit to The Monastery and Friary of St Francis, Gorton.

The Monastery Manchester. Gorton Lane Manchester M12 5WF Pugin's Former Franciscan Monastery was officially listed as one of the most endangered sites in the world, alongside the Taj Mahal, and the ruins of Pompeii. A restoration costing £6.5 million has produced an inspiring venue for weddings, conferences, spiritual reflection, arts, music, and other social and cultural occasions.

The monastery is open to the public from 12.00pm until 4pm on most Sundays. Refreshments are available in the Friars Pantry.

Concerts and other special events take place every week, and guided tours are also available. There are at least seven Sundays each year when it will not be open to the public. It is essential therefore, before you visit, to check the web page, http://www.themonastery.co.uk/Whats-on.html, or contact the team by email at events@the monastery.co.uk, or by phone on 0161 223 3211.

© OpenStreetMap contributors - opendatacommons.org

Getting There
By Car:
From Debdale Outdoor Centre, turn left out of the car park onto Wall Way. At the first lights go ahead to cross the A57.

Immediately, at the next set of lights, turn right onto the A57, Hyde Road towards Manchester. After 1.36 miles turn right onto the A1060 Inner Ring Road, and follow the brown tourist Monastery signs and look out for the green spire. After just under a mile you will arrive at St Francis Monastery, with its free car park, [**SFM**] on your left-hand side.

From Manchester, take the A635 Ashton Old Road, or A57 Hyde Road, to the A1060 Inner Ring Road. Turn there following the brown tourist Monastery signs and look out for the green spire.

From the M60, at junction 24 follow the A57 into Manchester. At the A6010 Inner Ring Road turn right and follow the Monastery signs, looking out for the green spire.

By Rail;
From Manchester Piccadilly Station take either a 5 minute taxi journey or the 205 Bus (which takes 10 minutes) and stops directly outside The Monastery.

"They crossed the car park and the front of the wall enclosing the cloistered garden, and stood before the four wooden doors and soaring buttresses of the Gothic red-brick, stone and Welsh slate church.

'Back in 1997, when it was declared one of the most endangered buildings in the world and given World Monument status, they nicknamed this Manchester's Taj Mahal.'

Holmes regarded the grotesque gargoyles staring back at him from the ledges beside each door.

'Doesn't do it for me,' he muttered. 'Anyway, how come you know so much about this place?'

'Two reasons,' Caton replied. 'I came here with Manchester Grammar School on a local history trip in the early eighties, just before the friars left.'

He started up the steps, closely followed by his DI.

'Two reasons, you said?'

'Kate and I are getting married here in two and a half weeks' time,' he replied, without breaking stride. 'You should read your invitation.'

Even Holmes had to admit that the inside was impressive. Beneath the ribbed vault of the ceiling, the nave was set out for a wedding. Soft pink lights illuminated the towering stone pillars, the choir, altar and the apse. Without warning, the light changed to blue, mottled with purple where the pointed arches reached the first and second storeys. It was like a vast film set for a gothic movie."

Backwash

Postscript:

Some Gorton Facts:

During the nineteenth century and the first half of the twentieth century Gorton was a major contributor to Manchester's industrial reputation, with two locomotive manufacturers producing engines for the global market, and attracting machine tool and other ancillary industries. For over a hundred and sixty years Belle Vue hosted the country's first true theme park. With its parks, circus, zoo, amusement park, King's Hall concert venue, boxing, wrestling, motorcycle speedway, stock car and greyhound racing, it was the playground of choice for hundreds of thousands of people every year from across Northern England and the North Midlands.

Shifting economic realities, changing tastes, and new technologies, saw a dramatic decline in manufacturing and employment during the third quarter of the 20th century. At Belle Vue only the motorcycle and greyhound racing remain, unless you include a multiplex cinema and ten pin bowling. To add insult to injury, the Moors Murderers, Ian Brady and Myra Hindley, worked together in Gorton, and were still here at the time of their arrest. The first four series of the critically acclaimed TV show Shameless, featuring the feckless Gallagher family, and the equally obnoxious fictional Chatsworth estate, was filmed right here. The notoriety that these two unrelated events attracted was in no way representative of the hardworking and moral majority, and was strongly resented.

Now the tide is turning. Initially left in the shadows of its neighbour – Eastlands – which benefited from hosting the 2002 Commonwealth Games in the form of the Etihad Stadium, the National Cycling Centre at the Velodrome, thousands of brand new houses and apartments, an Industrial Park, and modern transport facilities including metrolink stations - Gorton is on the move. It hosts a state of the art Sports Village, the main campus of Manchester College, and the New Smithfield Market. The West Gorton Development Plan is bringing much needed community facilities including a new medical centre, retail park, a new community park, relocation of council services, and a thousand new homes. This in an already resilient community which supported the restoration of St Francis Monastery, and won £450,000 from the Government's Inspiring Communities Programme.

It seems that the Gorton Monastery Voice Choir, supported by the Gorton Philharmonic Orchestra founded in 1854 and still going strong, really does have something to sing about.

Walk 8
West Pennines Country Park - Rivington

Associated Titles: A Fatal Intervention

The Walk

A Fascinating walk at any time of the year. A perfect half day excursion. Rivington, and its associated reservoirs nestle beneath the West Pennine Moors.   Formerly part of Lord Leverhulme's estate, in includes two ancient tithe barns, a folly – Liverpool Castle – and the remains of the terraced Chinese Gardens constructed along the hillside.   Several Bronze Age tumuli, or burial sites – have been found on the hilltops. A perfect setting for a crime novel.

Getting There:

From the M61 junction 6 follow signs for Bolton Centre. At The Beehive roundabout for the A673 turn left to Horwich. After almost two miles go straight ahead at next main roundabout and then turn immediate right between a pair of stone pillars onto Rivington Lane. After a further mile and a half you will see the Great House Barn and Visitor Centre car park on the left. You could park here, although the car park is always very busy. Instead, turn immediate right towards Rivington Hall and Barn, and park in the first available space. You will then be at point A on the map.

Distance:

Total Distance: 4,055 metres / 2.5 miles.
Total Walking Time: 1 Hour 25 Minutes

Allow the same amount of time again for exploration of the castle, deviation to the beach, pausing on the benches beside the reservoir, visiting the Great House Barn and Visitor Centre, and refreshments at the Rivington Village Tea Rooms.

Terrain: Generally flat but with some uneven surfaces, and steps. Boots or walking shoes advised, especially after heavy rain when small sections of some paths may be muddy. Take care when crossing roads. Do not enter the water in the reservoir. The reservoir supplies drinking water to homes, and the water is always exceptionally cold and can be treacherous.

Access issues: Sections of the walk are suitable for accompanied wheelchairs, and mobility scooters, but only when the paths are dry. Please check at the Great House Information Centre for details. Tel: 01204 691549

Map: OS Explorer 287 West Pennine Moors
Postcode for Rivington Village Tea Rooms [B on Map] BL6 7SD

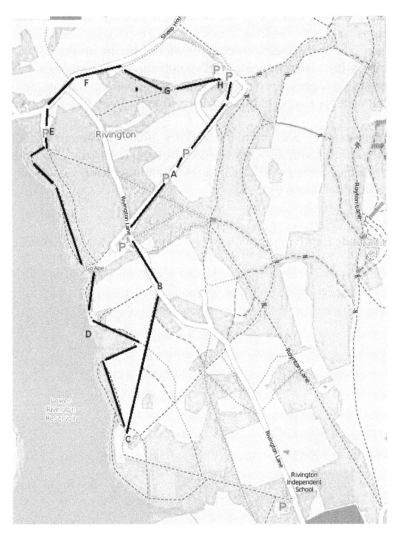

© OpenStreetMap contributors - opendatacommons.org

Start On the tree lined road opposite Great Hall Barn, leading to Rivington Hall and Rivington Barn (**A**). Leave your car and head back down the road, via a path beside the trees on the left hand side, towards Great Hall Barn. Take care crossing the road, and turn left, past the Great House Information Centre. After **2 minutes** arrive at a marked bridle path on your right **(B).**

This is the point at which DCI Caton began his fated trek though the snow to Liverpool Castle – see Extract.

"Even before he reached the barrier he could see that there were two sets of footprints heading away down the path ahead; one large, one smaller. He stopped and began searching either side of the path. On the path to the right of the track he found what he was looking for beneath the trees – a single set of the footprints, the larger of the two, returning. An icy fear took hold of him and he began to run."

A Fatal Intervention.

There are two paths at this point. Take the one directly ahead of you that leads past a wooden barrier across the track, in a long straight line. In Autumn you may see large clusters of yellow fungi growing on mounds of birch sawdust placed there by the park rangers.

After 10 minutes arrive at Liverpool Castle - the ruined folly built for Lord Leverhulme. **(C)**

"Three times he fell on the frozen ruts, smearing his coat with muddy slush, grazing the palms of his hands, bruising his knees and elbows. Each time he scrambled to his feet and hurried on. Within half a mile he could see the outline of a ruined castle through the bare branches. Where the track rose towards the imposing stone walls he caught a glimpse beyond them of steel-blue moonlit water beneath a lowering sky.

He reached the first of a series of rounded towers and slowed to walking pace. His chest was heaving, his throat burning. Each exhalation of breath sent a cloud of steam into the frosty air. High above his head, pairs of arrow slits in the curtain wall stared down like sightless eyes. He followed the wall around to the right until he reached three huge blocks of stone strewn in front of an opening in the wall, beyond which a Roman arch marked the entrance to a roofless courtyard. He stood still and listened for a moment. The only sound was the mournful cry of a bird out on the reservoir. He took a deep breath and walked towards the arch.

A breach in the wall at the farthest side of the ruins exposed a group of Canada geese bobbing on the troubled surface of the lake. To the right, three Gothic archways were set into buildings composed of thick blocks of the same grey millstone as the castle walls. The two pairs of footprints he had been following traced a path towards the central arch. The single set returned from the same direction.

Rob put his hand inside his coat and withdrew the tyre lever. It was so cold and his hand so wet with sweat, that he worried it might freeze to his palm and burn the skin. Logic told him that whoever it was he thought this weapon might protect him from was long gone. And yet he clung to it, just as he clung to a forlorn hope that he would find her alive.

Still conscious of the need to preserve the evidence, instead of following the trail under the archway he moved to his left and climbed a small bank to reach a narrow window through which he was able to see inside. The building consisted of a roofless circular enclosure. Propped against the far wall, facing the doorway, was a body covered from head to foot in a veil of snow. The head slumped forward. Thick red blood had congealed on top of the skull and was crimson upon the chest. Rob felt his legs going from under him. He clung to the wall for support and retched into the virgin snow. A pair of swans, disturbed by the sound, lifted off from the reservoir behind him and flew gracefully away."

A Fatal Intervention.

Take a little time to explore the ruins, but take care not to climb on any of the walls. This was the crime scene referred to in the extract above. Perhaps you can identify the exact spot where the body was found.

Retrace your steps to the entrance and, turning right, follow the path that skirts the castle. There are several short slopes, and flights of steps, that lead around the outside of the castle, beside the reservoir. Continue to follow the path for 10 minutes as it winds along the bank of the reservoir until you reach the point where the path splits into two. (**D**).

Take the left hand path and continue to follow it through the trees along the edge of the reservoir. Cross a small wooden bridge over a stream, and follow a four barred wooden fence up hill. On your right among the trees note the *Go Ape* platforms and zip wires that inspired the opening section of another of my books - *The Cave*. Take time to explore the little coves and beaches that border the reservoir, and take a moment to sit on one of the many benches to admire the view. Both great spots for a picnic. Follow another wooden fence uphill to arrive at the car park above Rivington Foundation Primary school **(E).** 14 minutes for this leg.

Descend the car park, and turn right onto Horrobin Lane. Walk uphill past the school arriving at a fork in the road. TAKE CARE. This is a blind bend. Ensure that you can see in all directions before crossing the road and climbing three steps onto the village green. Cross the green towards the church, and pass through the churchyard to arrive at Rivington Village Tea Rooms [**F**) [5 minutes].

Having taken well deserved refreshment, turn right outside the tea rooms onto Sheephouse Lane, and continue uphill for 100 yards, arriving at a footpath sign immediately after Chapel House. [2 minutes]. Take the right hand gravelled path, beyond the kissing gate, that leads across a young plantation which is a memorial arboretum. After 8 minutes, emerge onto a broad lane [**G**].

Turn left and head gently uphill to arrive in 9 minutes at Rivington Hall Barn (**H**). Fortnightly, on Wednesdays, this historic Saxon barn hosts antique and collectors fairs. At weekends, expect to see hordes of motorbike enthusiasts both here and at the Great House Barn, where they are joined by droves of cyclists.

Facing the entrance to the barn, turn right, and walk round to the impressive frontage of Rivington Hall. The last time that

I was here a peacock was sitting on the balustrade. Continue down the curved drive, turning right onto the straight, broad tree lined road where you parked your car **(A)**.

Acknowledgements

I have to start with Liz Welsh, who tired of waiting for me to begin this book, began to plan her own walks based on the novels, and spurred me into action. My wife Joan, who is a Mancunian, and who accompanied me on most of the planning expeditions. Alan Wheatley, and Barbara and Carlton Caterall who offered to act as guinea pigs to check out the finished walks.

Then there are the staff of all of the key sites and attractions who provided up to date information, especially about access for wheelchair users, and others with access needs. Manchester Cathedral, Chetham Library, The Royal Exchange, St Anne's Church, The Rylands Library, Manchester Town Hall, The Portico, Central Library, Manchester Museum, Manchester University, Christie Library and Bistro, The Whitworth Gallery, Manchester City Art Gallery, The National Football Museum, MOSI, the Air and Space Museum, Imperial War Museum North, The Lowry Theatre and Gallery, The Old Nag's Head, The Rising Sun, The Salutation Inn.

Useful Links

If these walks have whetted your appetite, these links cover organisations that offer detailed guided walks in the city around special themes.

http://www.newmanchesterwalks.com/

http://www.visitmanchester.com/what-to-do/walkstours/

http://www.manchesterguidedtours.com/

http://www.walkmanchester.com/

If you would like to read more about Manchester a good place to start would be the following excellent street by street guide: The Manchester Compendium, by Ed Glinert. ISBN 9780141029306

The Author

Bill Rogers has written nine crime thriller novels to date – all of them based in and around the City of Manchester. His first novel *The Cleansing* received the ePublishing Consortium Writers Award 2011, and was short listed for the Long Barn Books Debut Novel Award. His Fourth novel, *A Trace of Blood, reached* the semi-final of the Amazon Breakthrough Novel Award in 2009.

Bill has also written *Breakfast at Katsouris,* an anthology of short crime stories, and a novel for teens, young adults and adults, called *The Cave.* He lives in Greater Manchester where he has spent his entire adult life.

www.billrogers.co.uk

www.catonbooks.com

List of DCI Tom Manchester Murder Mysteries in order

The Cleansing

The Head Case

The Tiger's Cave

A Fatal Intervention

A Trace of Blood

Bluebell Hollow

The Frozen Contract

Backwash

A Venetian Moon

All of his books are available as paperbacks from bookshops, or on Amazon, and as Amazon Kindle EBooks